1ST LEGION OF UTOPIA

Written by
James Davidge

Character Art by
Bob Prodor

Background Art & Colours by
Nick Johnson

Colour Flats by
Kyle Burles

Lettered by
Ryan Ferrier

RENEGADE
ARTS ENTERTAINMENT

1st Legion of Utopia is a work of fiction. All incidents and dialogue, and all characters, locations and businesses with the exception of recognized historical figures, locations and businesses, are products of the author's imagination and are not to be construed as real. Any resemblance to actual persons, living or dead, or actual events are purely coincidental.

Published by Renegade Arts Canmore Ltd trading as
Renegade Arts Entertainment

Renegade Arts Canmore Ltd
President: John Finbow Publisher: Alexander Finbow
Business Development: Luisa Harkins Marketing: Sean Tonelli
Reporting & Asset Management: Emily Pomeroy
www.renegadeartsentertainment.com

Office of business:
Renegade Arts Canmore Ltd, 25 Prospect Heights, Canmore,
Alberta T1W 2S2 email: contact@renegademail.com

First edition
Softcover ISBN : 9781988903545
ebook ISBN: 9781988903606

Printed in Canada by Friesens

Supported by the Government of Alberta

Alberta Foundation for the Arts

MIX
Paper from responsible sources
FSC® C016245

Alberta Government

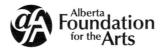

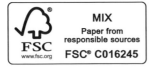

PART I
A PROTEST OF SILENT SUFFERERS

"The State is to make what is useful. The individual is to make what is beautiful."

- Oscar Wilde

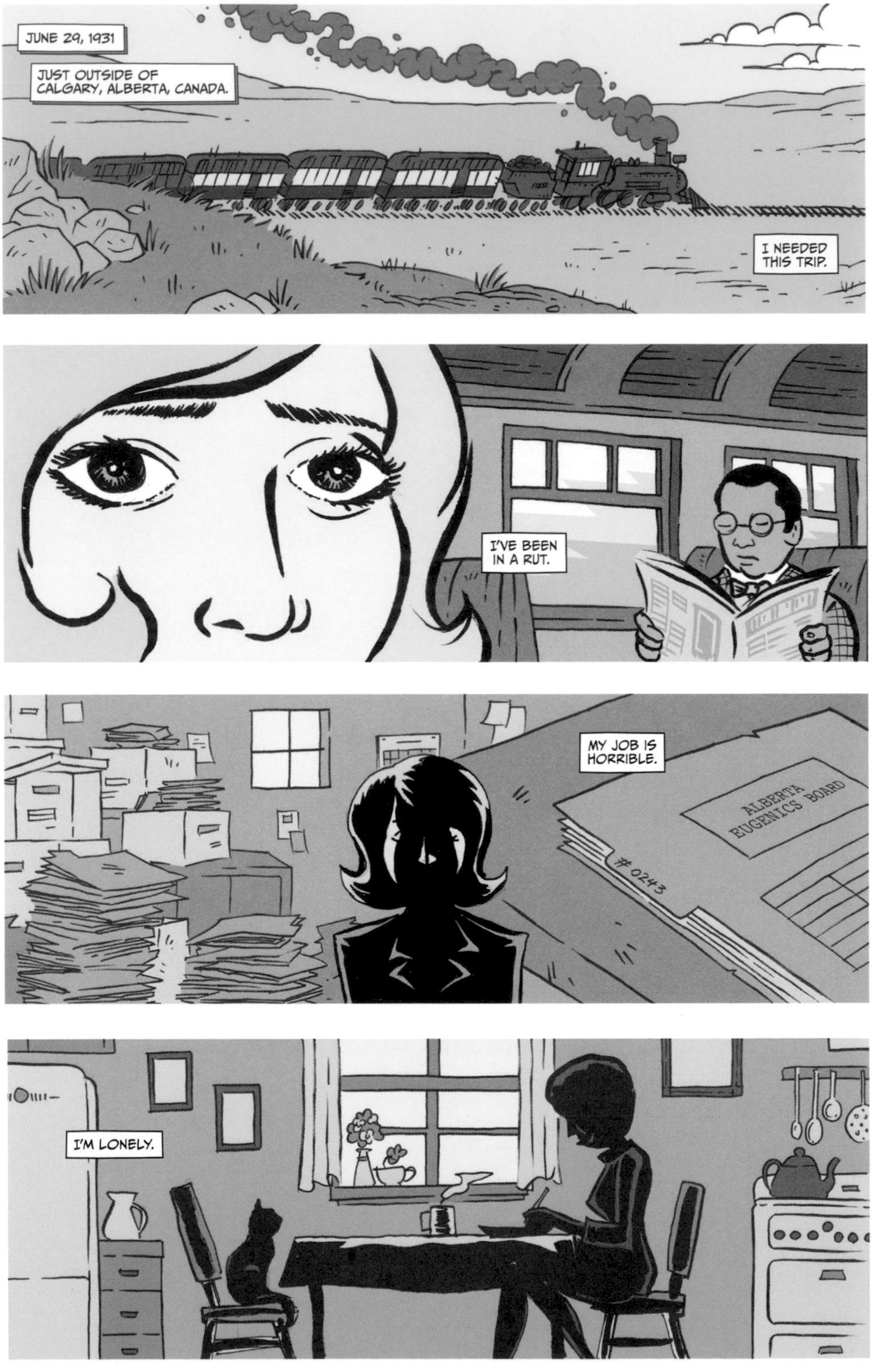
JUNE 29, 1931
JUST OUTSIDE OF CALGARY, ALBERTA, CANADA.
I NEEDED THIS TRIP.
I'VE BEEN IN A RUT.
MY JOB IS HORRIBLE.
ALBERTA EUGENICS BOARD
#0243
I'M LONELY.

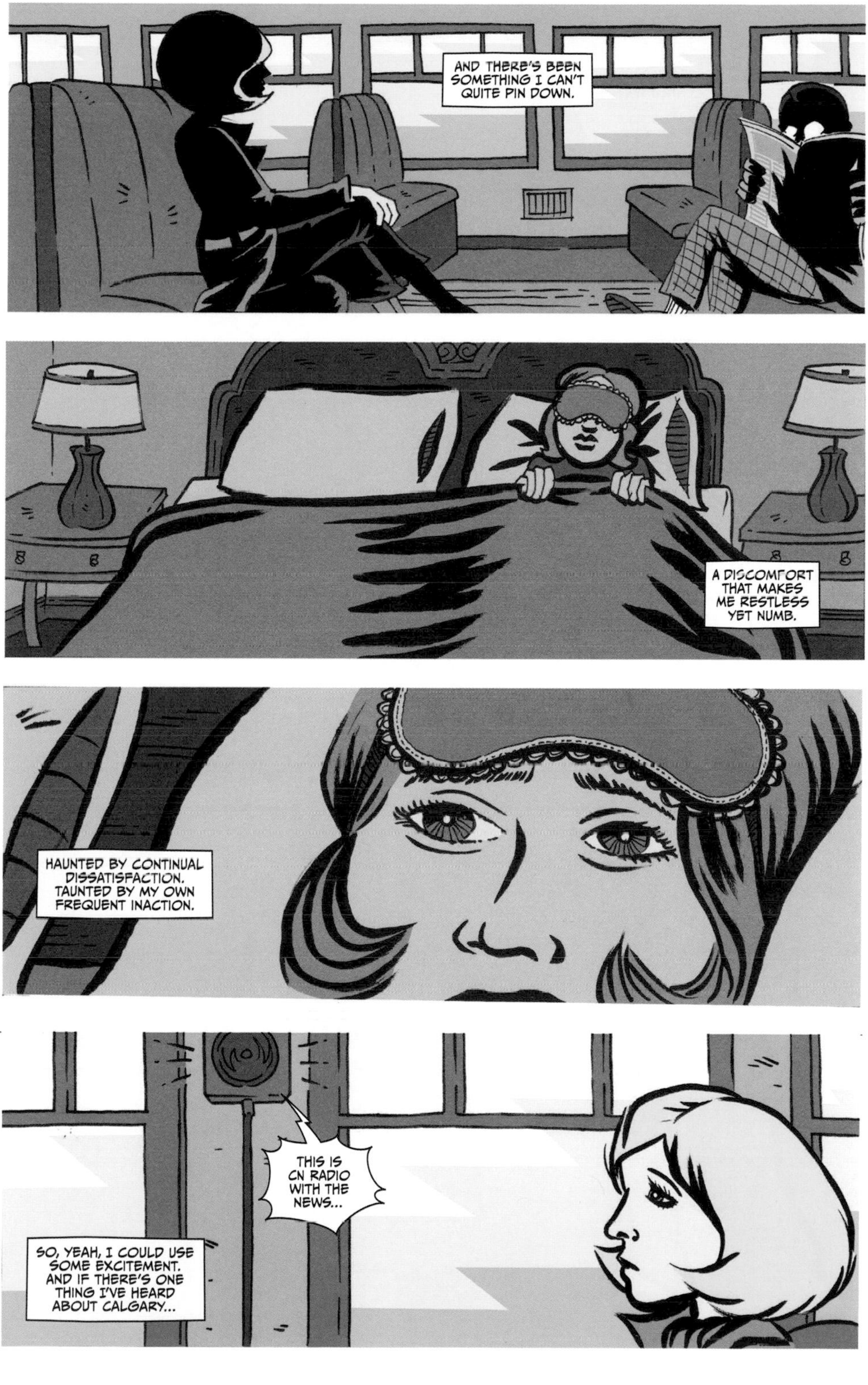
AND THERE'S BEEN SOMETHING I CAN'T QUITE PIN DOWN.
A DISCOMFORT THAT MAKES ME RESTLESS YET NUMB.
HAUNTED BY CONTINUAL DISSATISFACTION. TAUNTED BY MY OWN FREQUENT INACTION.
THIS IS CN RADIO WITH THE NEWS...
SO, YEAH, I COULD USE SOME EXCITEMENT. AND IF THERE'S ONE THING I'VE HEARD ABOUT CALGARY...

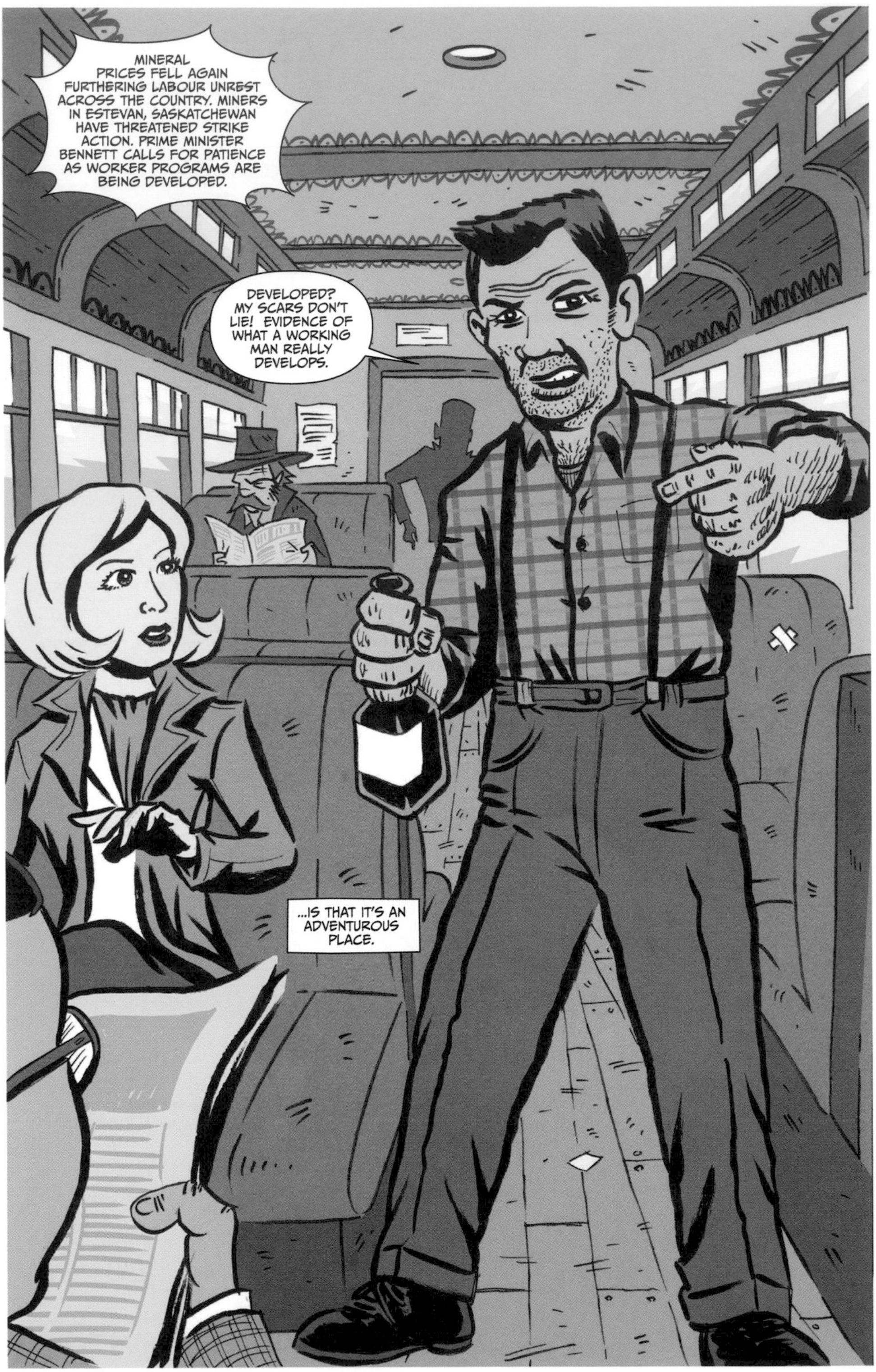
MINERAL PRICES FELL AGAIN FURTHERING LABOUR UNREST ACROSS THE COUNTRY. MINERS IN ESTEVAN, SASKATCHEWAN HAVE THREATENED STRIKE ACTION. PRIME MINISTER BENNETT CALLS FOR PATIENCE AS WORKER PROGRAMS ARE BEING DEVELOPED.
DEVELOPED? MY SCARS DON'T LIE! EVIDENCE OF WHAT A WORKING MAN REALLY DEVELOPS.
...IS THAT IT'S AN ADVENTUROUS PLACE.

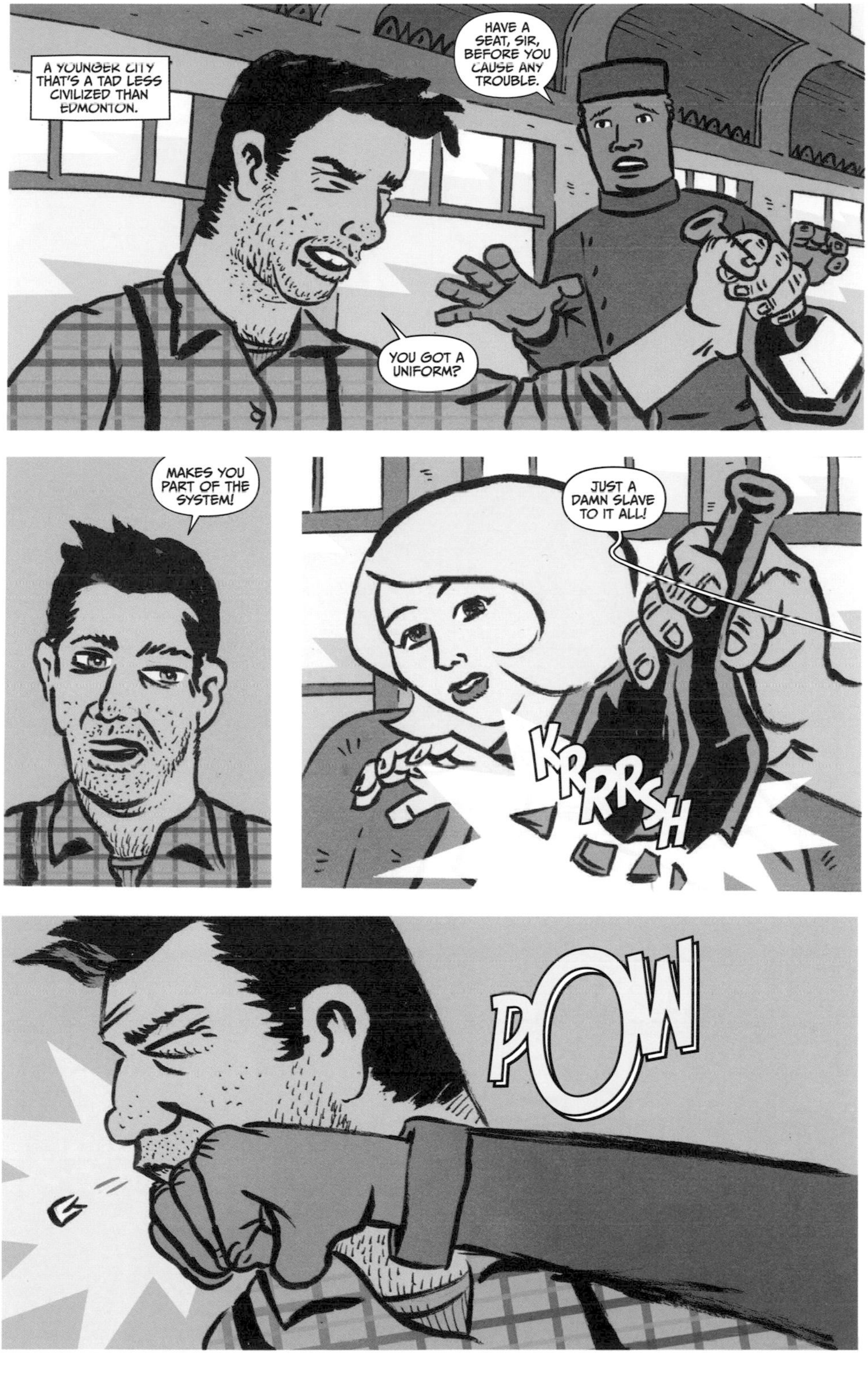
A YOUNGER CITY THAT'S A TAD LESS CIVILIZED THAN EDMONTON.
HAVE A SEAT, SIR, BEFORE YOU CAUSE ANY TROUBLE.
YOU GOT A UNIFORM?
MAKES YOU PART OF THE SYSTEM!
JUST A DAMN SLAVE TO IT ALL!
KRRRSH
POW

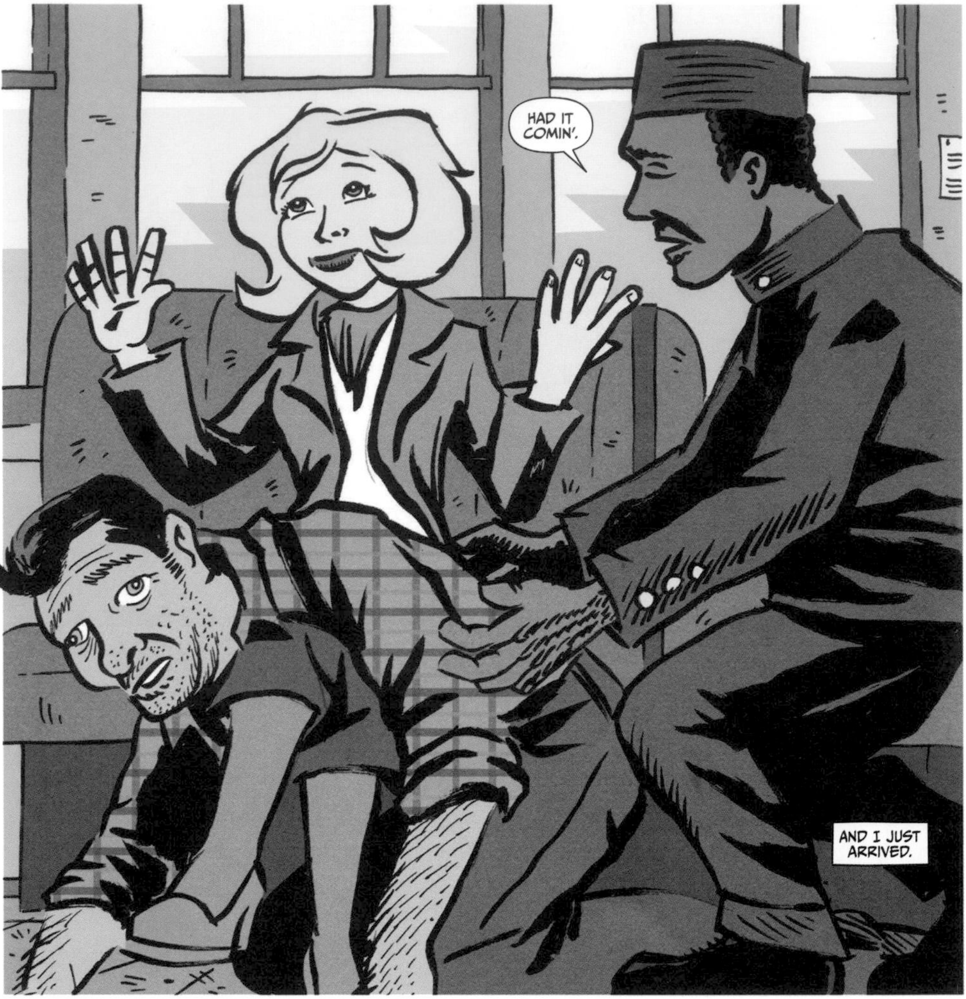
HAD IT COMIN'.
AND I JUST ARRIVED.

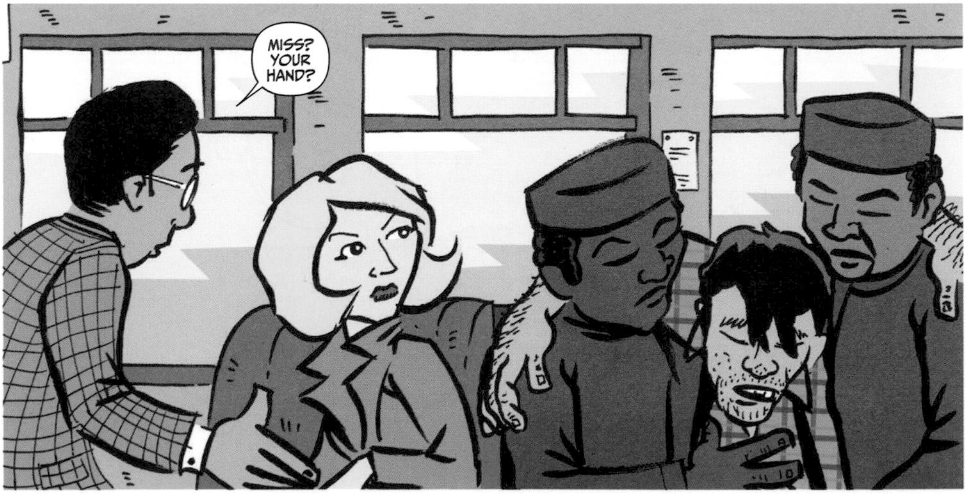
MISS? YOUR HAND?

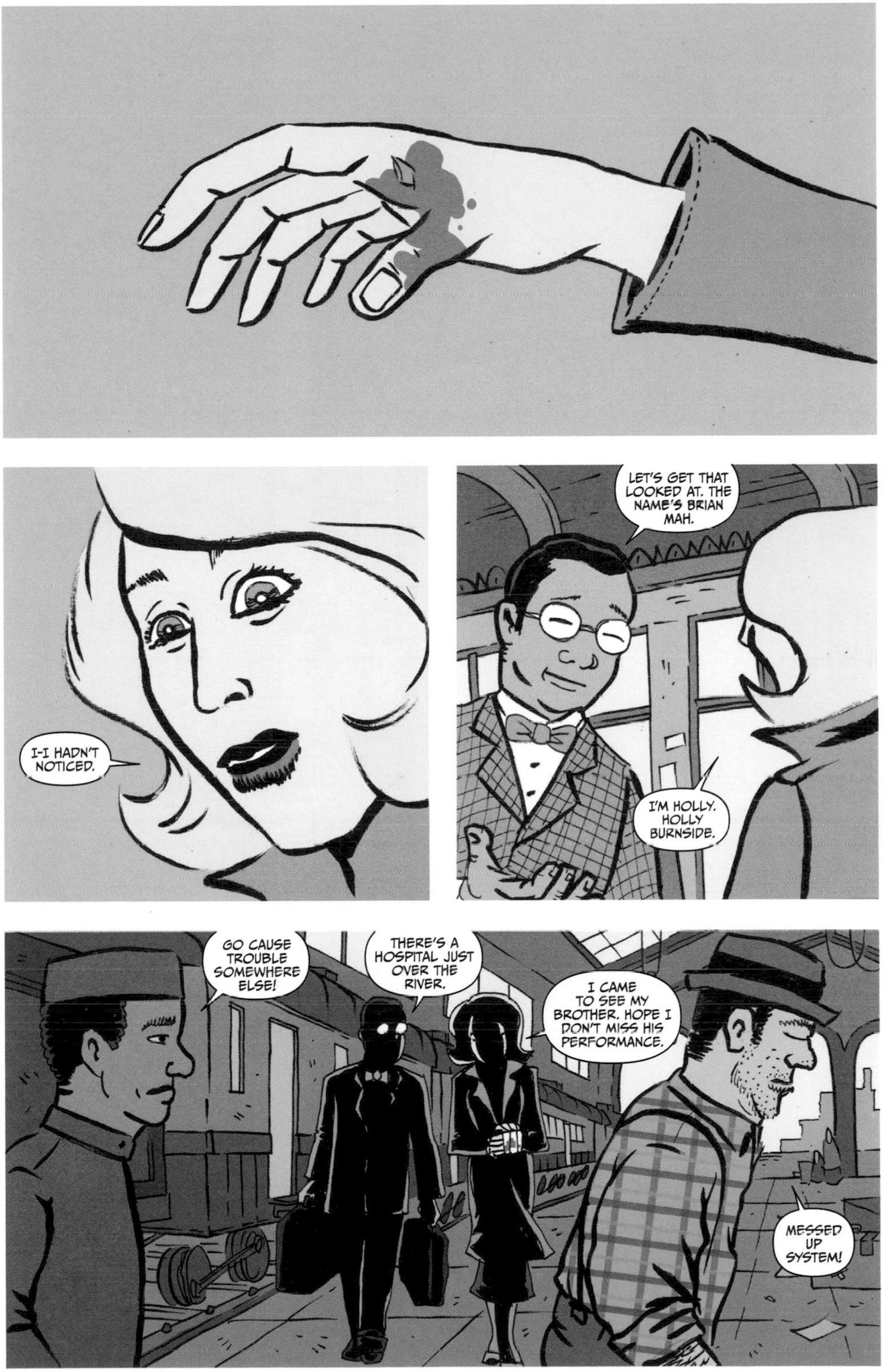
I-I HADN'T NOTICED.
LET'S GET THAT LOOKED AT. THE NAME'S BRIAN MAH.
I'M HOLLY. HOLLY BURNSIDE.
GO CAUSE TROUBLE SOMEWHERE ELSE!
THERE'S A HOSPITAL JUST OVER THE RIVER.
I CAME TO SEE MY BROTHER. HOPE I DON'T MISS HIS PERFORMANCE.
MESSED UP SYSTEM!

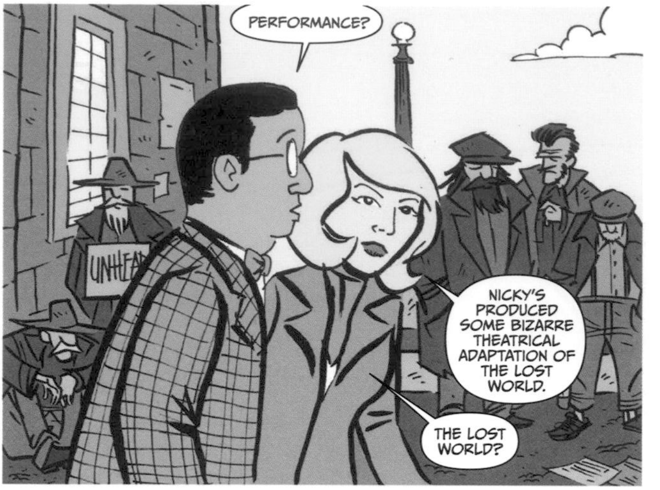
PERFORMANCE?
NICKY'S PRODUCED SOME BIZARRE THEATRICAL ADAPTATION OF THE LOST WORLD.
THE LOST WORLD?

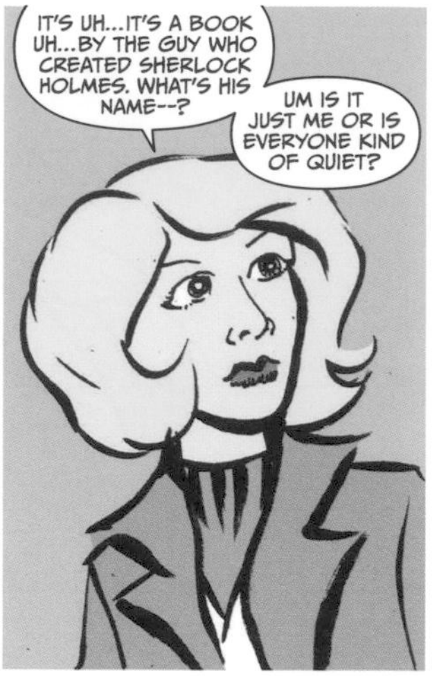
IT'S UH...IT'S A BOOK UH...BY THE GUY WHO CREATED SHERLOCK HOLMES. WHAT'S HIS NAME--?
UM IS IT JUST ME OR IS EVERYONE KIND OF QUIET?

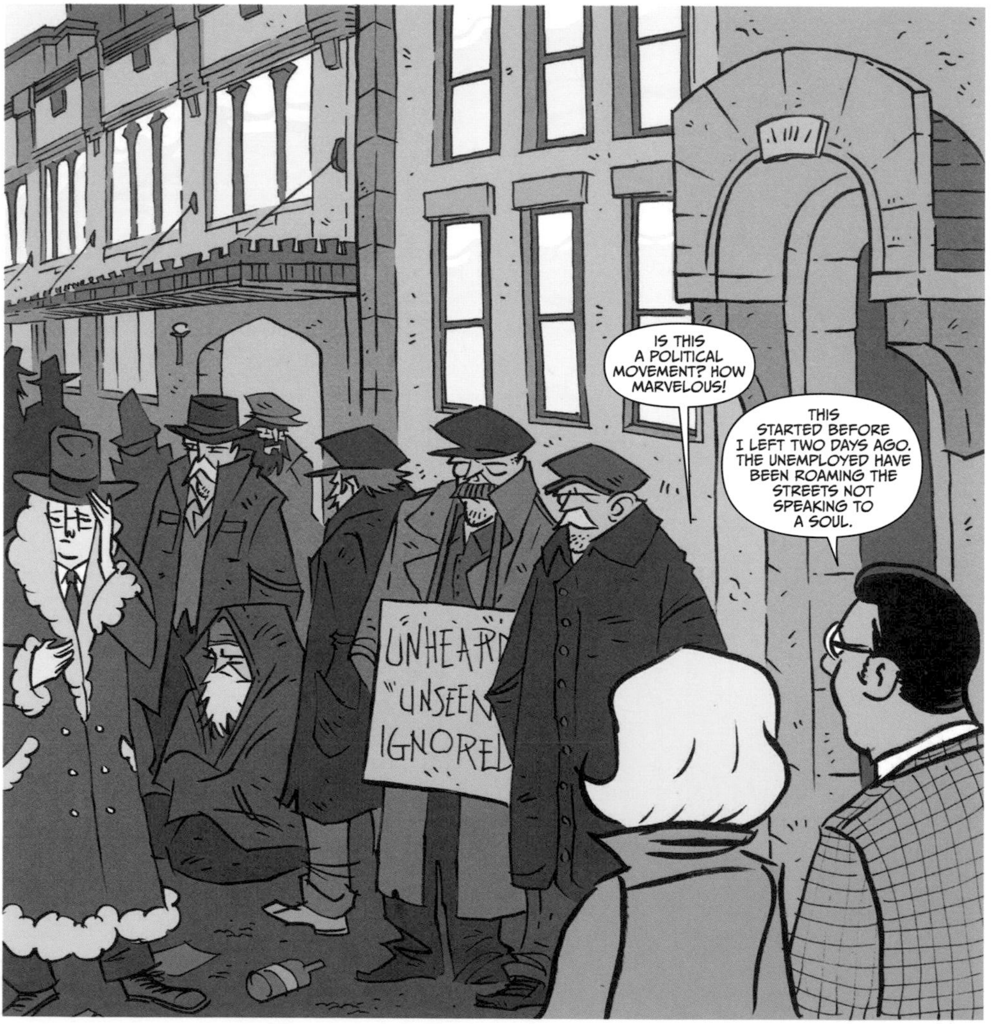
IS THIS A POLITICAL MOVEMENT? HOW MARVELOUS!
THIS STARTED BEFORE I LEFT TWO DAYS AGO. THE UNEMPLOYED HAVE BEEN ROAMING THE STREETS NOT SPEAKING TO A SOUL.

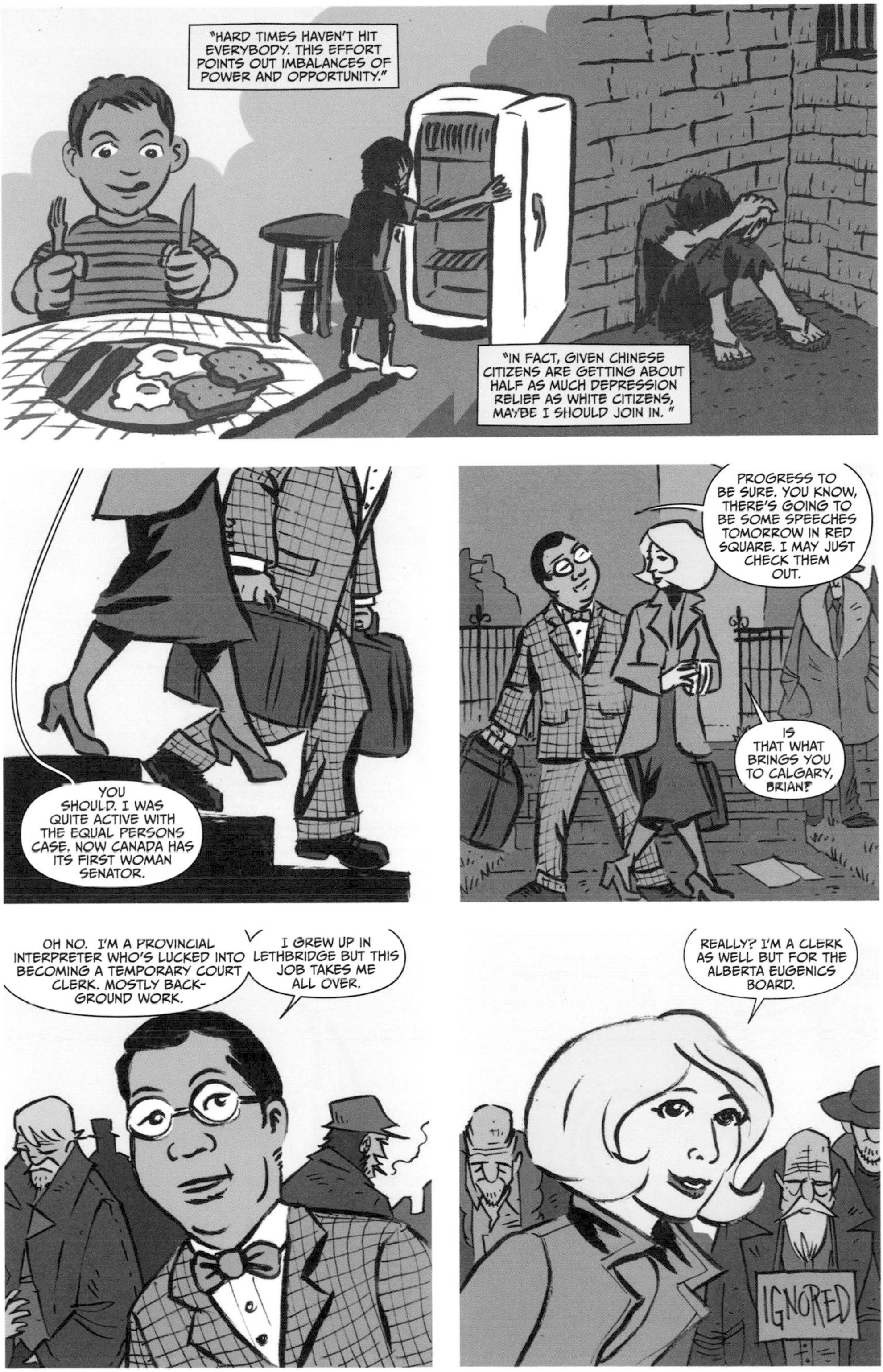
"HARD TIMES HAVEN'T HIT EVERYBODY. THIS EFFORT POINTS OUT IMBALANCES OF POWER AND OPPORTUNITY."
"IN FACT, GIVEN CHINESE CITIZENS ARE GETTING ABOUT HALF AS MUCH DEPRESSION RELIEF AS WHITE CITIZENS, MAYBE I SHOULD JOIN IN."
YOU SHOULD. I WAS QUITE ACTIVE WITH THE EQUAL PERSONS CASE. NOW CANADA HAS ITS FIRST WOMAN SENATOR.
PROGRESS TO BE SURE. YOU KNOW, THERE'S GOING TO BE SOME SPEECHES TOMORROW IN RED SQUARE. I MAY JUST CHECK THEM OUT.
IS THAT WHAT BRINGS YOU TO CALGARY, BRIAN?
OH NO. I'M A PROVINCIAL INTERPRETER WHO'S LUCKED INTO BECOMING A TEMPORARY COURT CLERK. MOSTLY BACK-GROUND WORK.
I GREW UP IN LETHBRIDGE BUT THIS JOB TAKES ME ALL OVER.
REALLY? I'M A CLERK AS WELL BUT FOR THE ALBERTA EUGENICS BOARD.
IGNORED

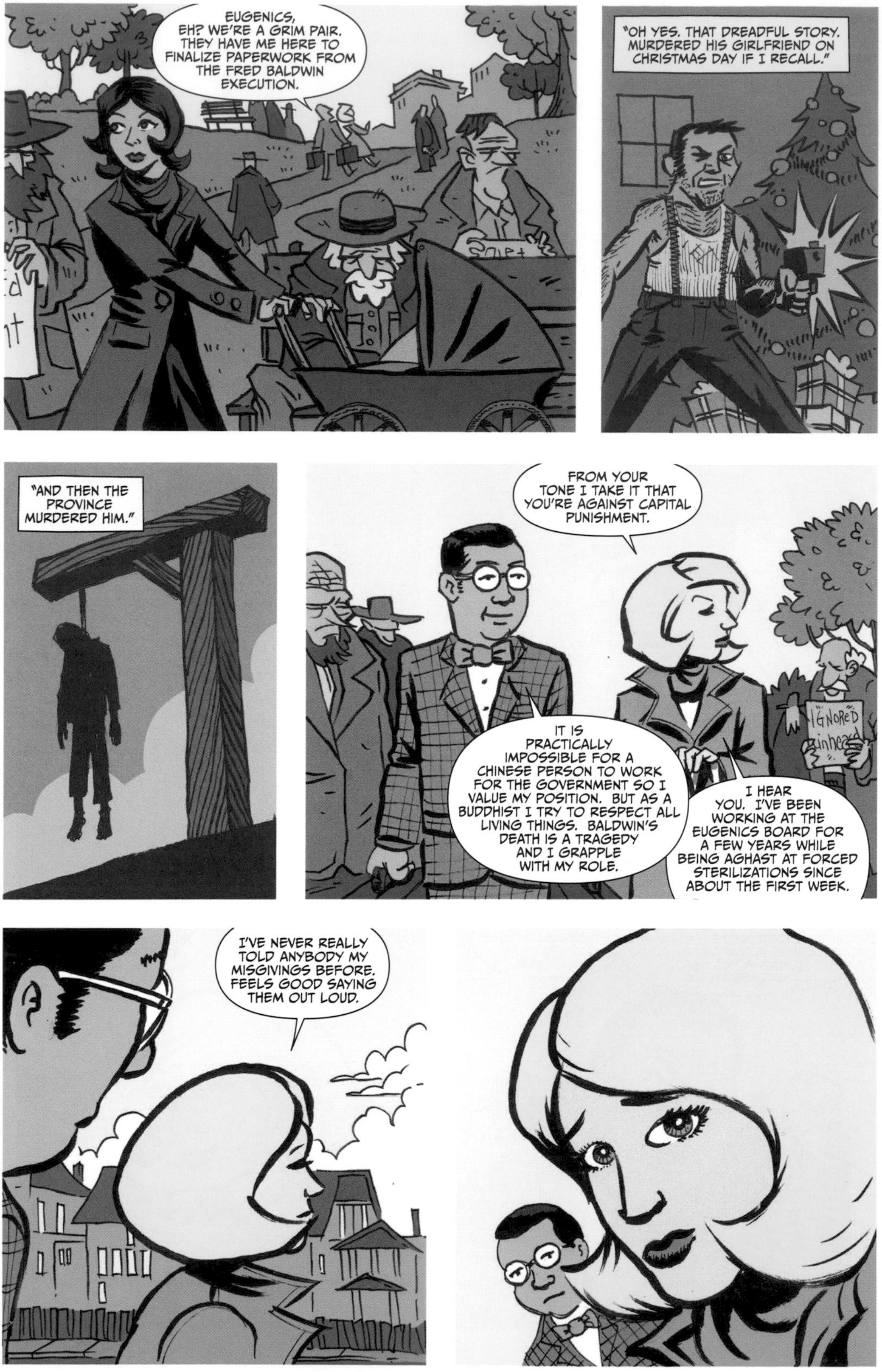
EUGENICS, EH? WE'RE A GRIM PAIR. THEY HAVE ME HERE TO FINALIZE PAPERWORK FROM THE FRED BALDWIN EXECUTION.
"OH YES. THAT DREADFUL STORY. MURDERED HIS GIRLFRIEND ON CHRISTMAS DAY IF I RECALL."
"AND THEN THE PROVINCE MURDERED HIM."
FROM YOUR TONE I TAKE IT THAT YOU'RE AGAINST CAPITAL PUNISHMENT.
IGNORED
IT IS PRACTICALLY IMPOSSIBLE FOR A CHINESE PERSON TO WORK FOR THE GOVERNMENT SO I VALUE MY POSITION. BUT AS A BUDDHIST I TRY TO RESPECT ALL LIVING THINGS. BALDWIN'S DEATH IS A TRAGEDY AND I GRAPPLE WITH MY ROLE.
I HEAR YOU. I'VE BEEN WORKING AT THE EUGENICS BOARD FOR A FEW YEARS WHILE BEING AGHAST AT FORCED STERILIZATIONS SINCE ABOUT THE FIRST WEEK.
I'VE NEVER REALLY TOLD ANYBODY MY MISGIVINGS BEFORE. FEELS GOOD SAYING THEM OUT LOUD.

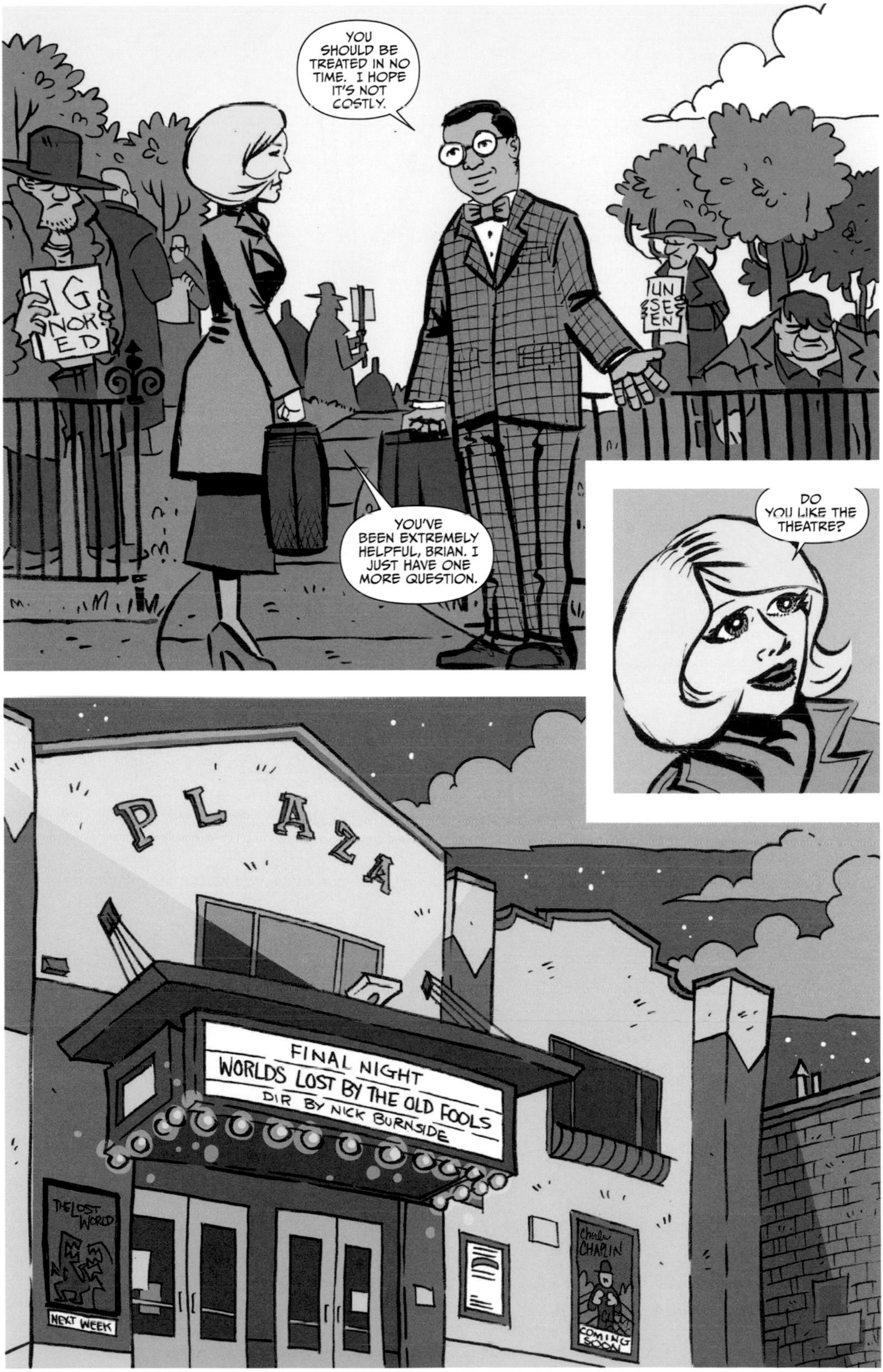
IG NORED
YOU SHOULD BE TREATED IN NO TIME. I HOPE IT'S NOT COSTLY.
UN SE EN
YOU'VE BEEN EXTREMELY HELPFUL, BRIAN. I JUST HAVE ONE MORE QUESTION.
DO YOU LIKE THE THEATRE?
PLAZA
FINAL NIGHT
WORLDS LOST BY THE OLD FOOLS
DIR BY NICK BURNSIDE
THE LOST WORLD
NEXT WEEK
CHAPLIN
COMING SOON

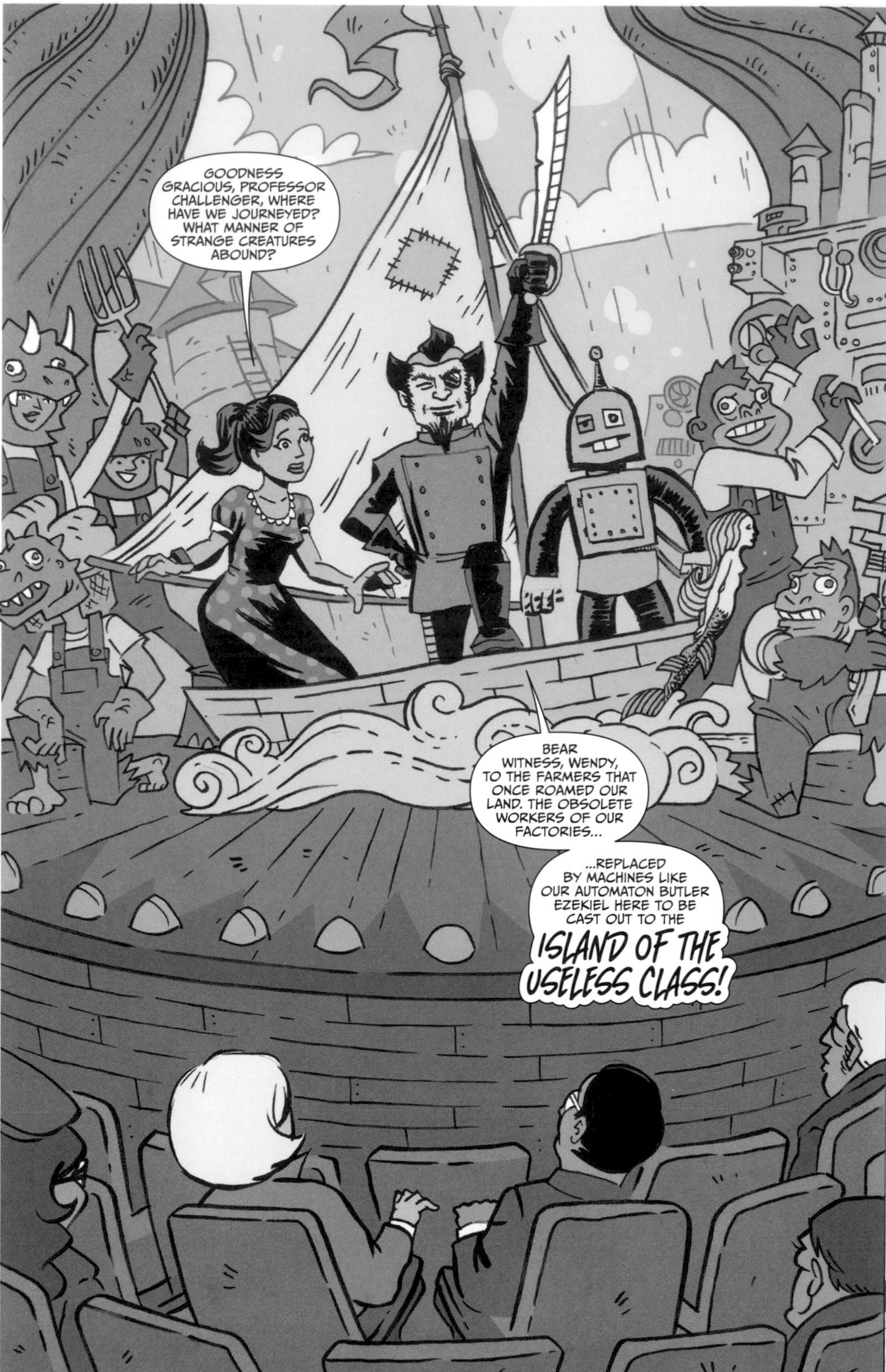
GOODNESS GRACIOUS, PROFESSOR CHALLENGER, WHERE HAVE WE JOURNEYED? WHAT MANNER OF STRANGE CREATURES ABOUND?
BEAR WITNESS, WENDY, TO THE FARMERS THAT ONCE ROAMED OUR LAND. THE OBSOLETE WORKERS OF OUR FACTORIES...
...REPLACED BY MACHINES LIKE OUR AUTOMATON BUTLER EZEKIEL HERE TO BE CAST OUT TO THE
ISLAND OF THE USELESS CLASS!

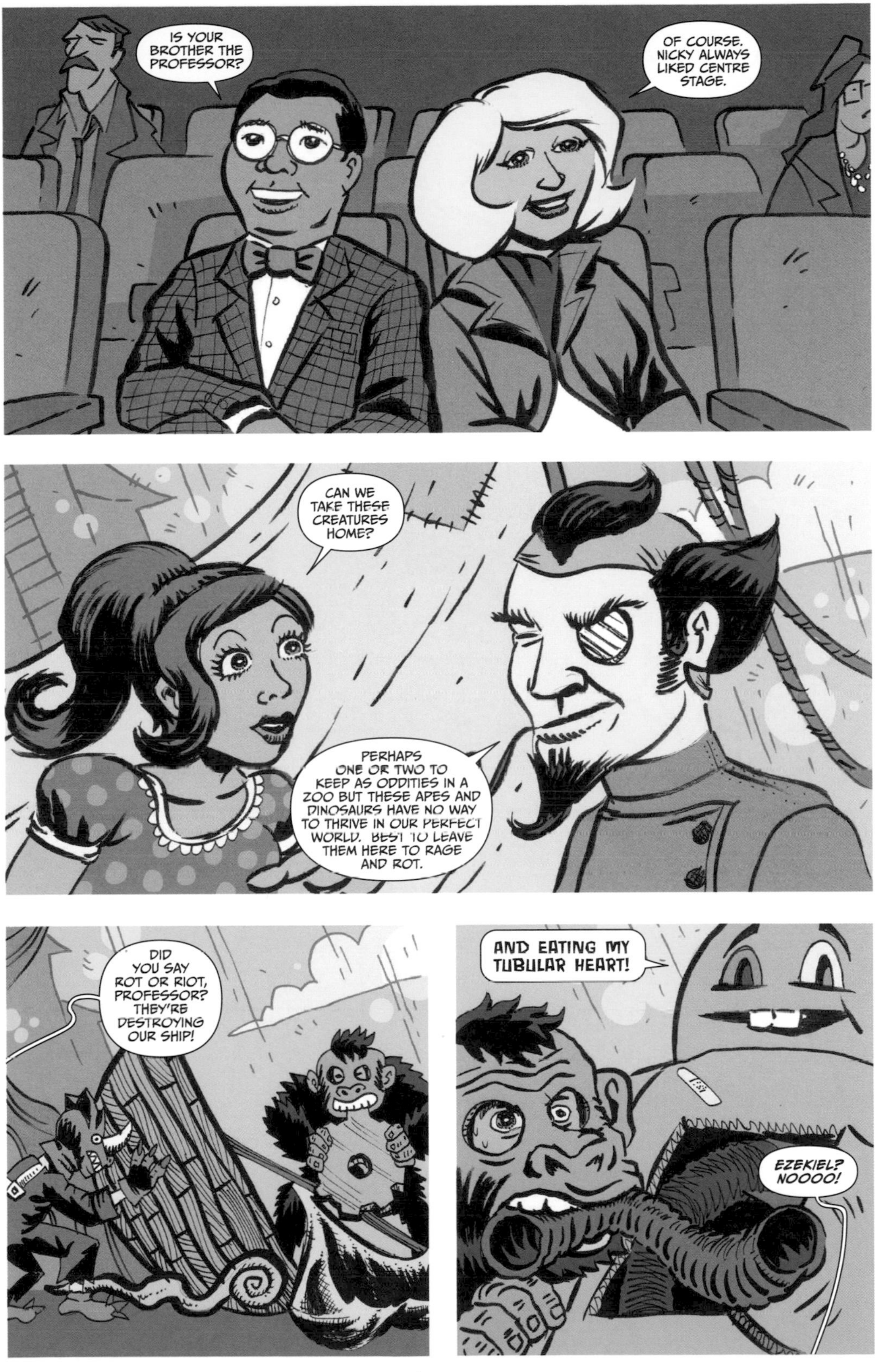
IS YOUR BROTHER THE PROFESSOR?
OF COURSE. NICKY ALWAYS LIKED CENTRE STAGE.
CAN WE TAKE THESE CREATURES HOME?
PERHAPS ONE OR TWO TO KEEP AS ODDITIES IN A ZOO BUT THESE APES AND DINOSAURS HAVE NO WAY TO THRIVE IN OUR PERFECT WORLD. BEST TO LEAVE THEM HERE TO RAGE AND ROT.
DID YOU SAY ROT OR RIOT, PROFESSOR? THEY'RE DESTROYING OUR SHIP!
AND EATING MY TUBULAR HEART!
EZEKIEL? NOOOO!

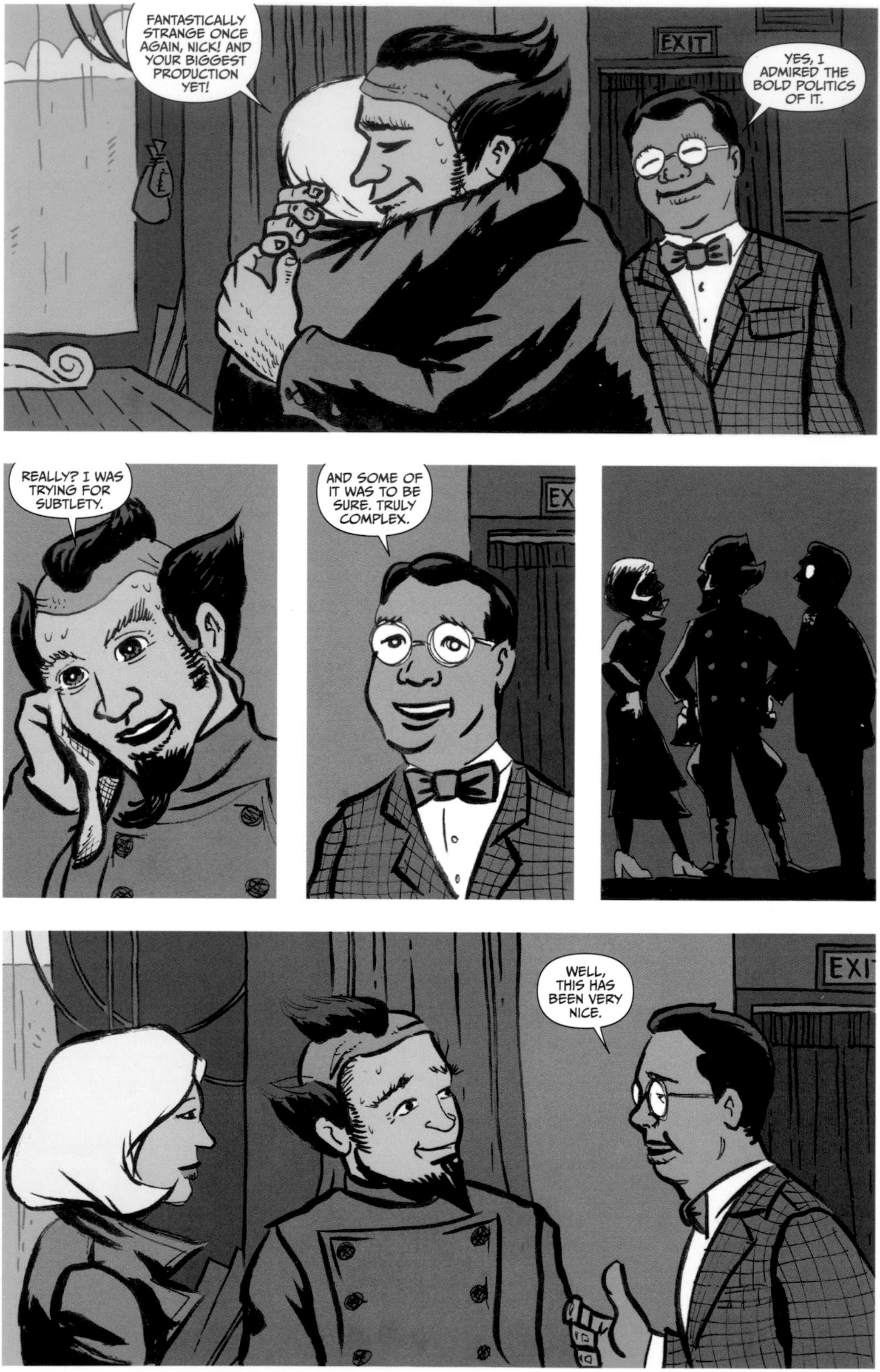
FANTASTICALLY STRANGE ONCE AGAIN, NICK! AND YOUR BIGGEST PRODUCTION YET!
EXIT
YES, I ADMIRED THE BOLD POLITICS OF IT.
REALLY? I WAS TRYING FOR SUBTLETY.
AND SOME OF IT WAS TO BE SURE. TRULY COMPLEX.
WELL, THIS HAS BEEN VERY NICE.

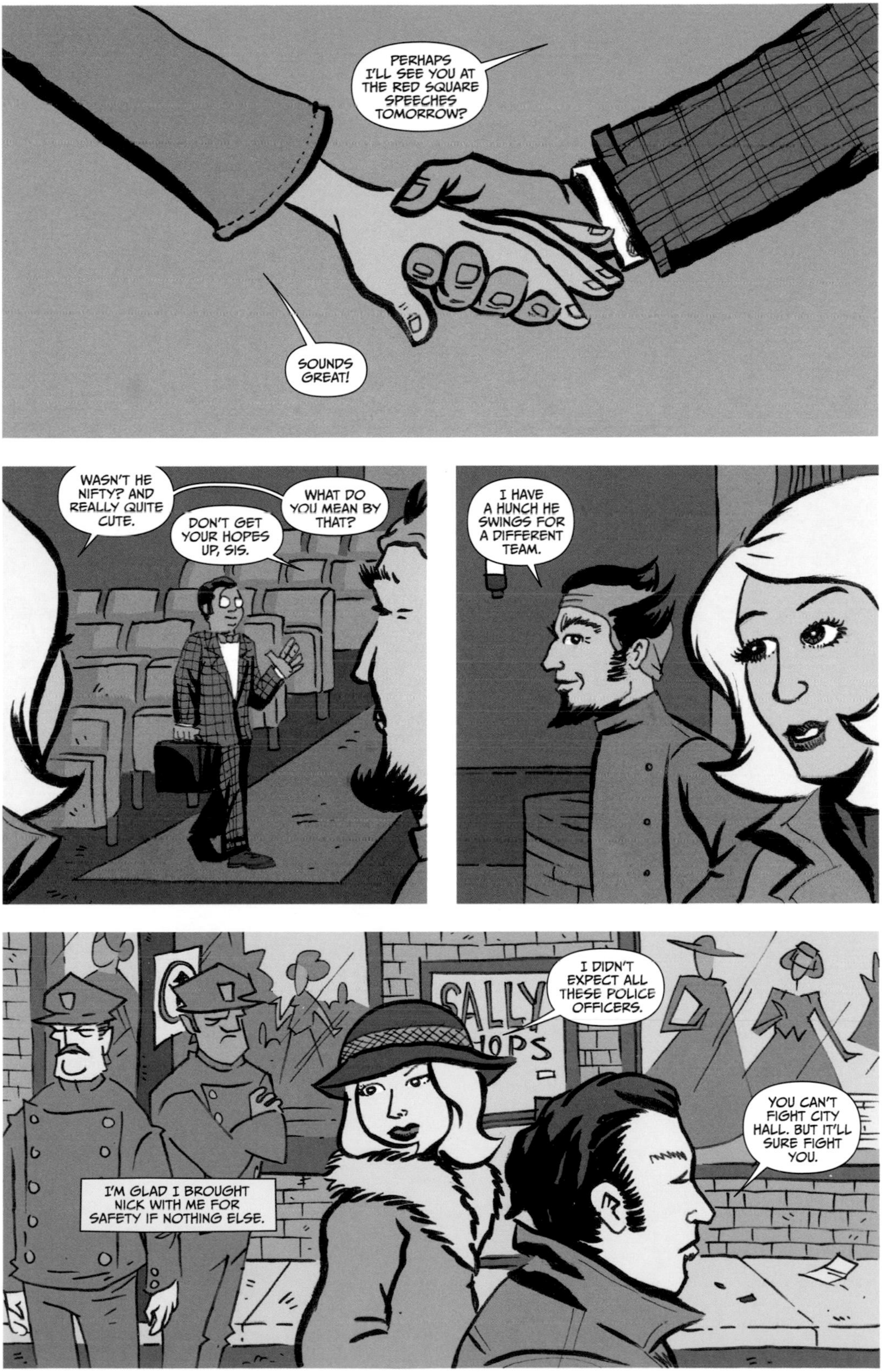
PERHAPS I'LL SEE YOU AT THE RED SQUARE SPEECHES TOMORROW?
SOUNDS GREAT!
WASN'T HE NIFTY? AND REALLY QUITE CUTE.
WHAT DO YOU MEAN BY THAT?
DON'T GET YOUR HOPES UP, SIS.
I HAVE A HUNCH HE SWINGS FOR A DIFFERENT TEAM.
I'M GLAD I BROUGHT NICK WITH ME FOR SAFETY IF NOTHING ELSE.
SALLY
OPS
I DIDN'T EXPECT ALL THESE POLICE OFFICERS.
YOU CAN'T FIGHT CITY HALL. BUT IT'LL SURE FIGHT YOU.

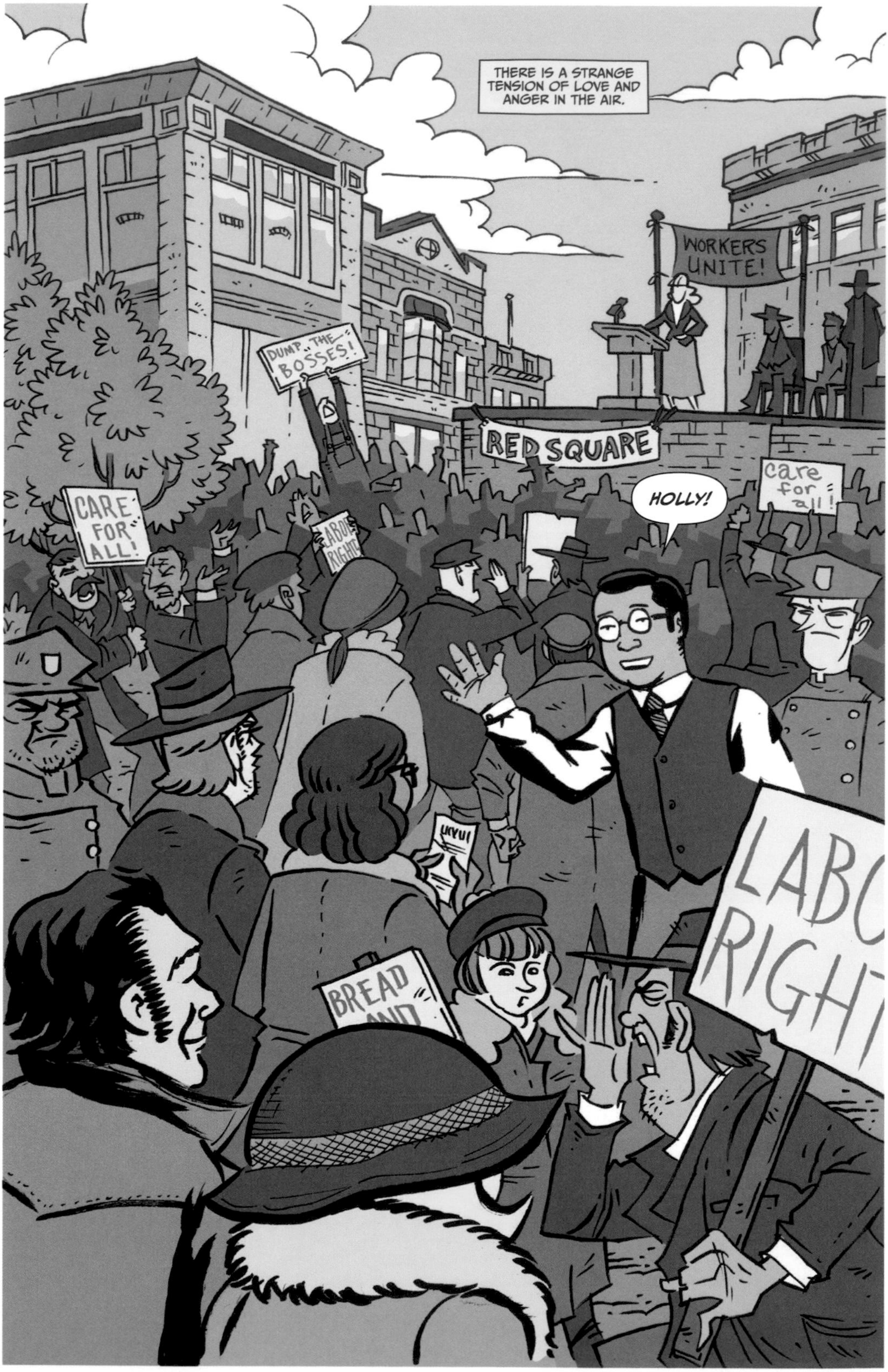
THERE IS A STRANGE TENSION OF LOVE AND ANGER IN THE AIR.
WORKERS UNITE!
DUMP THE BOSSES!
RED SQUARE
CARE FOR ALL!
care for all!
HOLLY!
BREAD

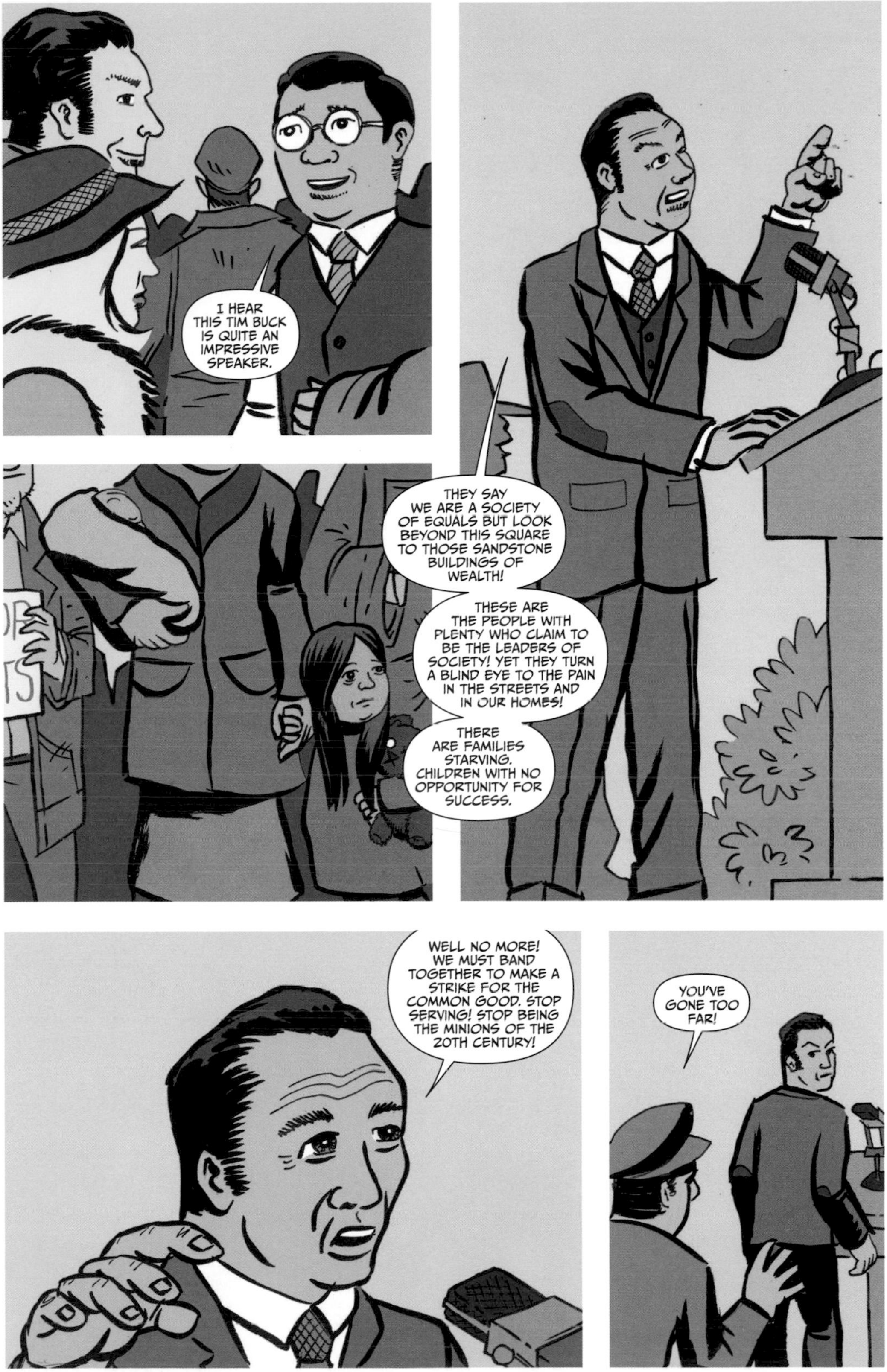
I HEAR THIS TIM BUCK IS QUITE AN IMPRESSIVE SPEAKER.
THEY SAY WE ARE A SOCIETY OF EQUALS BUT LOOK BEYOND THIS SQUARE TO THOSE SANDSTONE BUILDINGS OF WEALTH!
THESE ARE THE PEOPLE WITH PLENTY WHO CLAIM TO BE THE LEADERS OF SOCIETY! YET THEY TURN A BLIND EYE TO THE PAIN IN THE STREETS AND IN OUR HOMES!
THERE ARE FAMILIES STARVING. CHILDREN WITH NO OPPORTUNITY FOR SUCCESS.
WELL NO MORE! WE MUST BAND TOGETHER TO MAKE A STRIKE FOR THE COMMON GOOD. STOP SERVING! STOP BEING THE MINIONS OF THE 20TH CENTURY!
YOU'VE GONE TOO FAR!

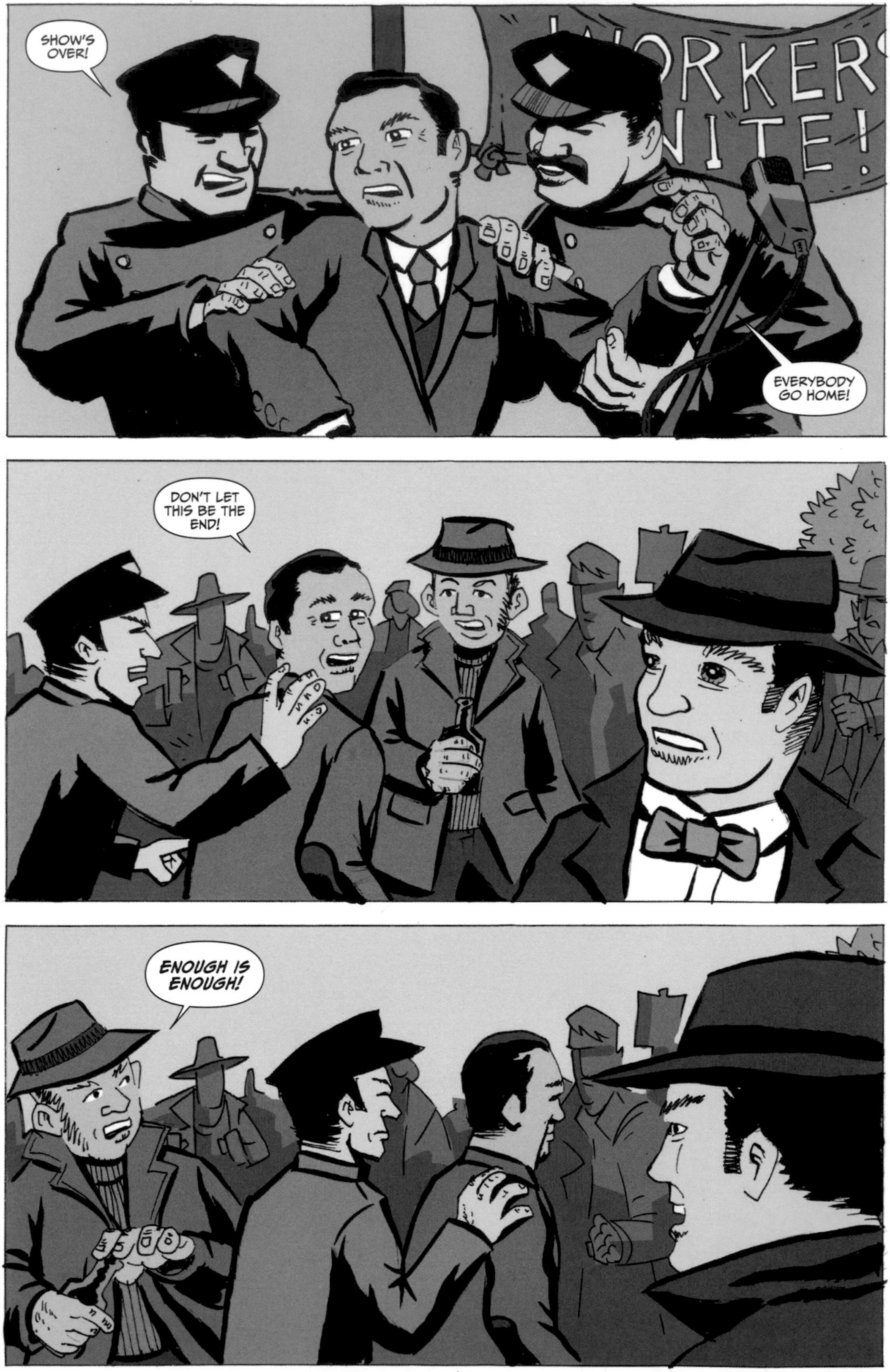
SHOW'S OVER!
ORKER
NITE!
EVERYBODY GO HOME!
DON'T LET THIS BE THE END!
ENOUGH IS ENOUGH!

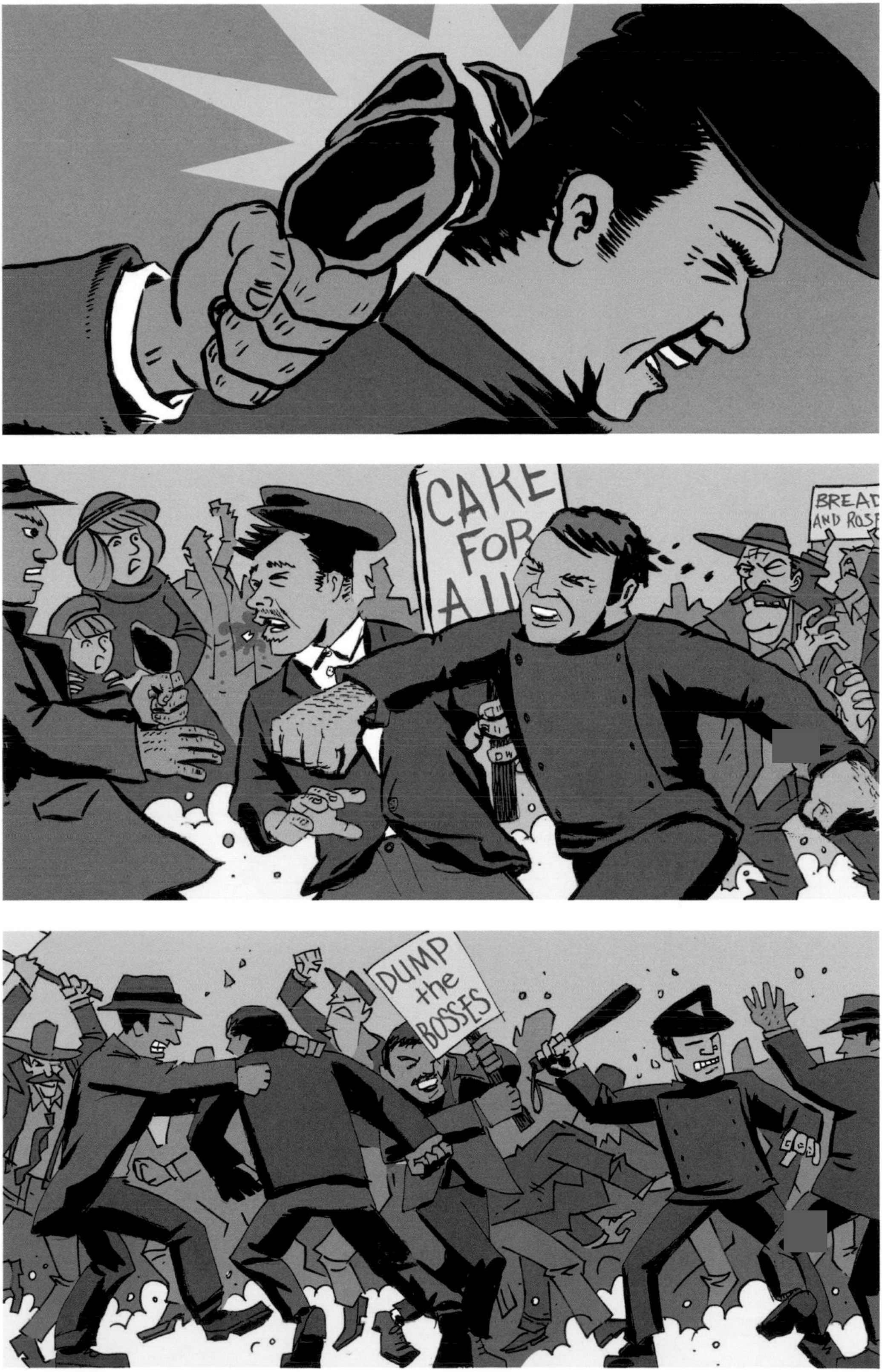
CARE
FOR
BREAD
DUMP the BOSSES

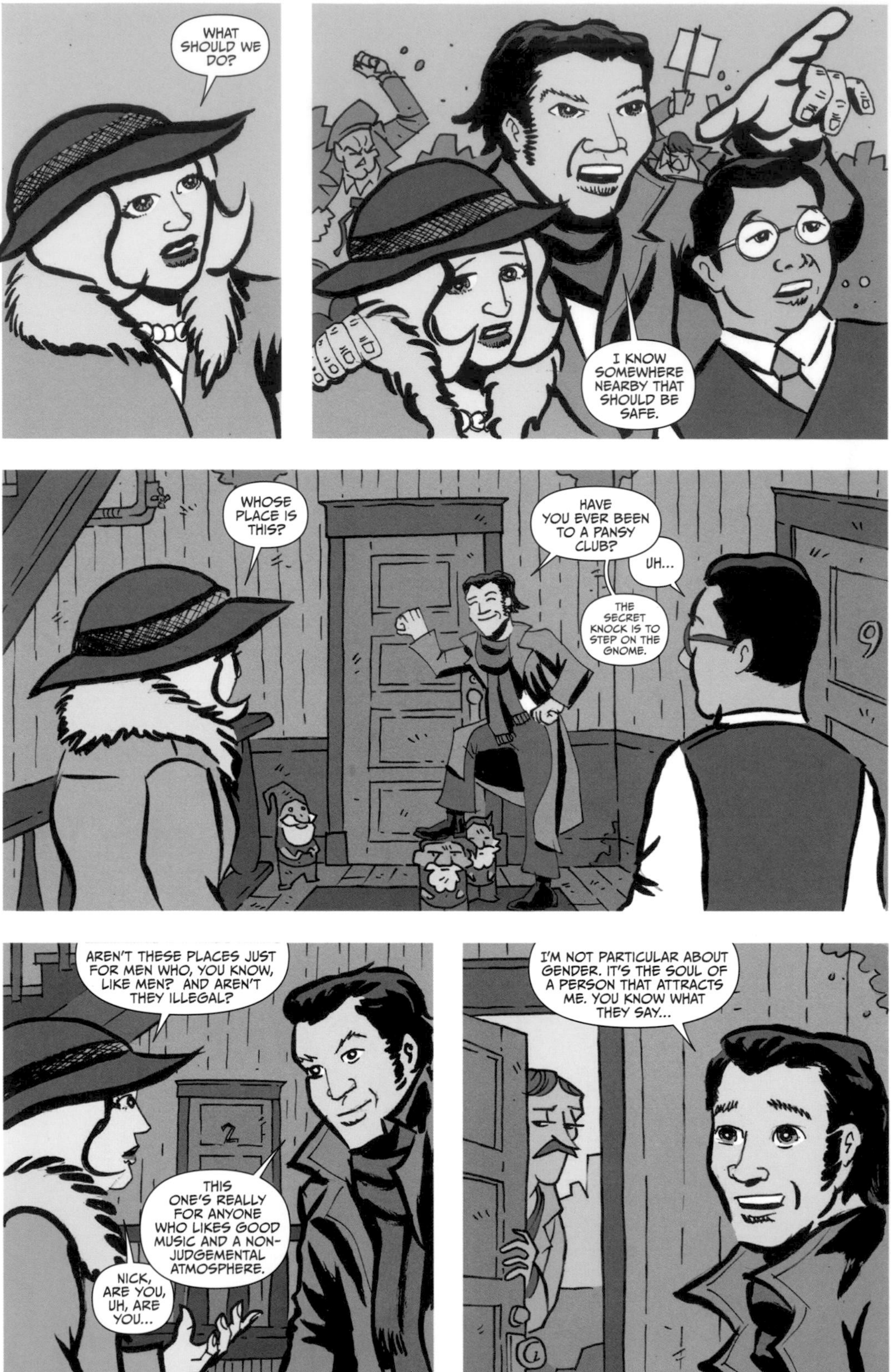
WHAT SHOULD WE DO?
I KNOW SOMEWHERE NEARBY THAT SHOULD BE SAFE.
WHOSE PLACE IS THIS?
HAVE YOU EVER BEEN TO A PANSY CLUB?
UH...
THE SECRET KNOCK IS TO STEP ON THE GNOME.
9
AREN'T THESE PLACES JUST FOR MEN WHO, YOU KNOW, LIKE MEN? AND AREN'T THEY ILLEGAL?
2
THIS ONE'S REALLY FOR ANYONE WHO LIKES GOOD MUSIC AND A NON-JUDGEMENTAL ATMOSPHERE.
NICK, ARE YOU, UH, ARE YOU...
I'M NOT PARTICULAR ABOUT GENDER. IT'S THE SOUL OF A PERSON THAT ATTRACTS ME. YOU KNOW WHAT THEY SAY...

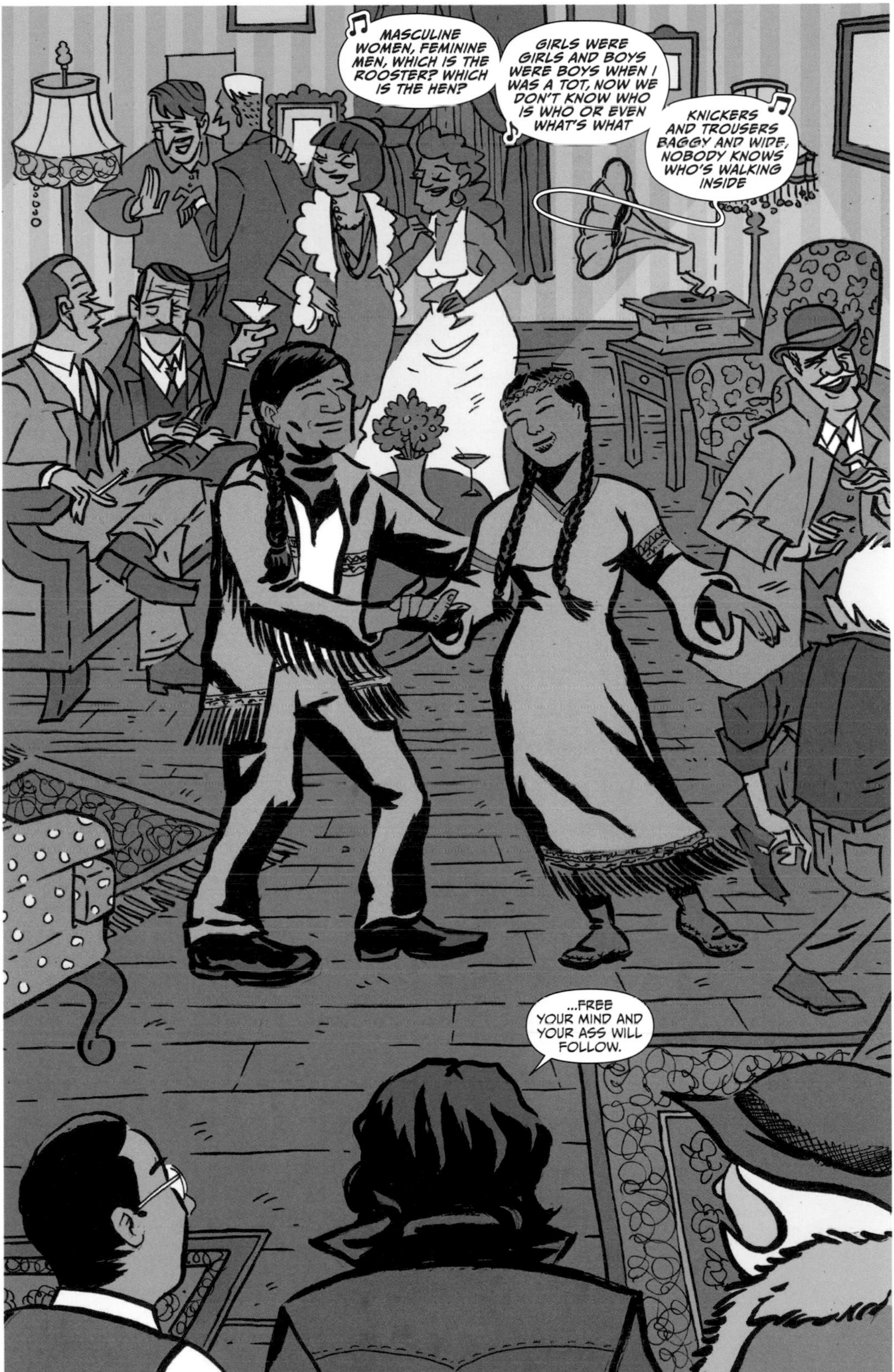
MASCULINE WOMEN, FEMININE MEN, WHICH IS THE ROOSTER? WHICH IS THE HEN?
GIRLS WERE GIRLS AND BOYS WERE BOYS WHEN I WAS A TOT, NOW WE DON'T KNOW WHO IS WHO OR EVEN WHAT'S WHAT
KNICKERS AND TROUSERS BAGGY AND WIDE, NOBODY KNOWS WHO'S WALKING INSIDE
...FREE YOUR MIND AND YOUR ASS WILL FOLLOW.

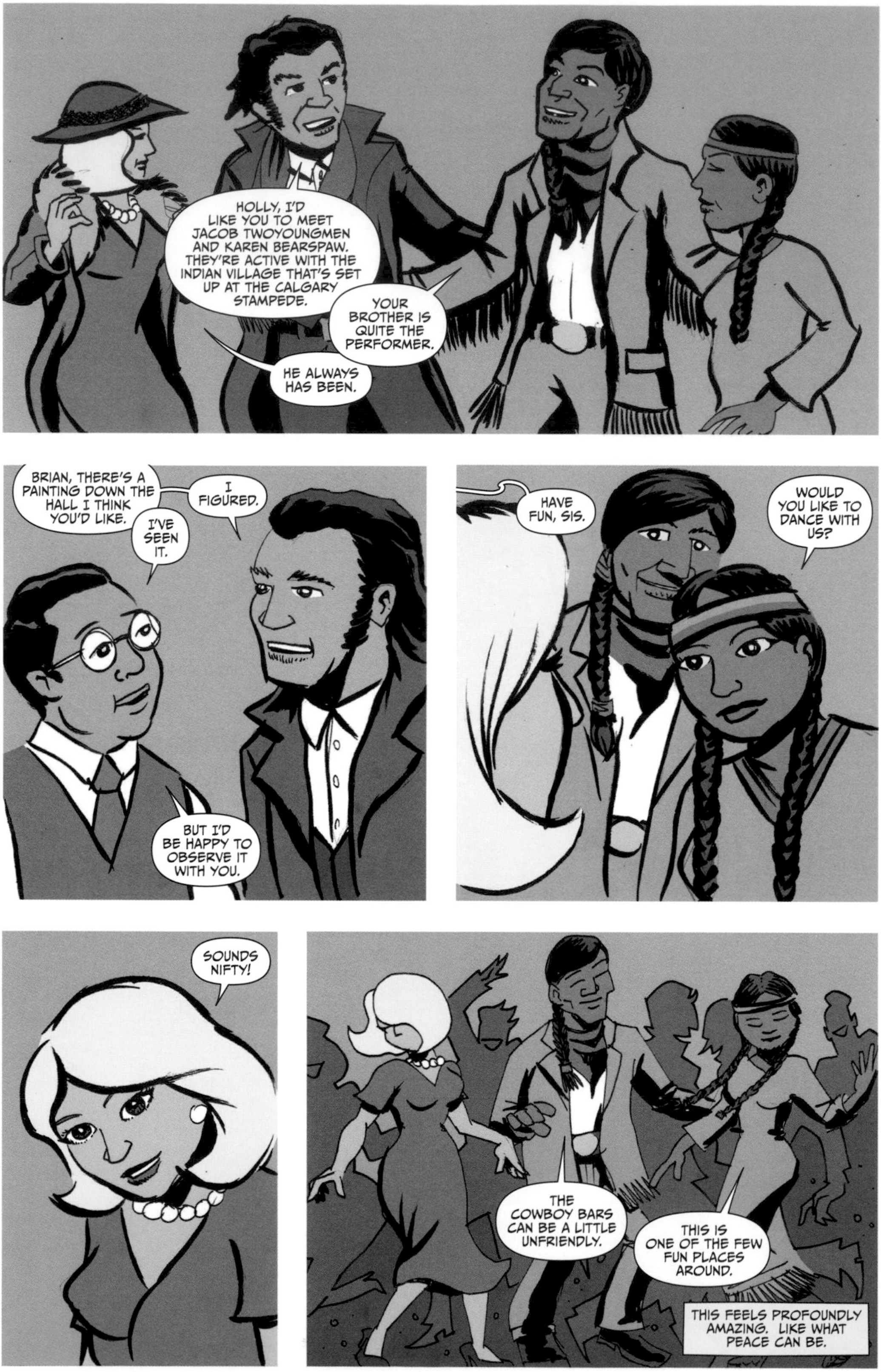
HOLLY, I'D LIKE YOU TO MEET JACOB TWOYOUNGMEN AND KAREN BEARSPAW. THEY'RE ACTIVE WITH THE INDIAN VILLAGE THAT'S SET UP AT THE CALGARY STAMPEDE.
YOUR BROTHER IS QUITE THE PERFORMER.
HE ALWAYS HAS BEEN.
BRIAN, THERE'S A PAINTING DOWN THE HALL I THINK YOU'D LIKE.
I FIGURED.
I'VE SEEN IT.
BUT I'D BE HAPPY TO OBSERVE IT WITH YOU.
HAVE FUN, SIS.
WOULD YOU LIKE TO DANCE WITH US?
SOUNDS NIFTY!
THE COWBOY BARS CAN BE A LITTLE UNFRIENDLY.
THIS IS ONE OF THE FEW FUN PLACES AROUND.
THIS FEELS PROFOUNDLY AMAZING. LIKE WHAT PEACE CAN BE.

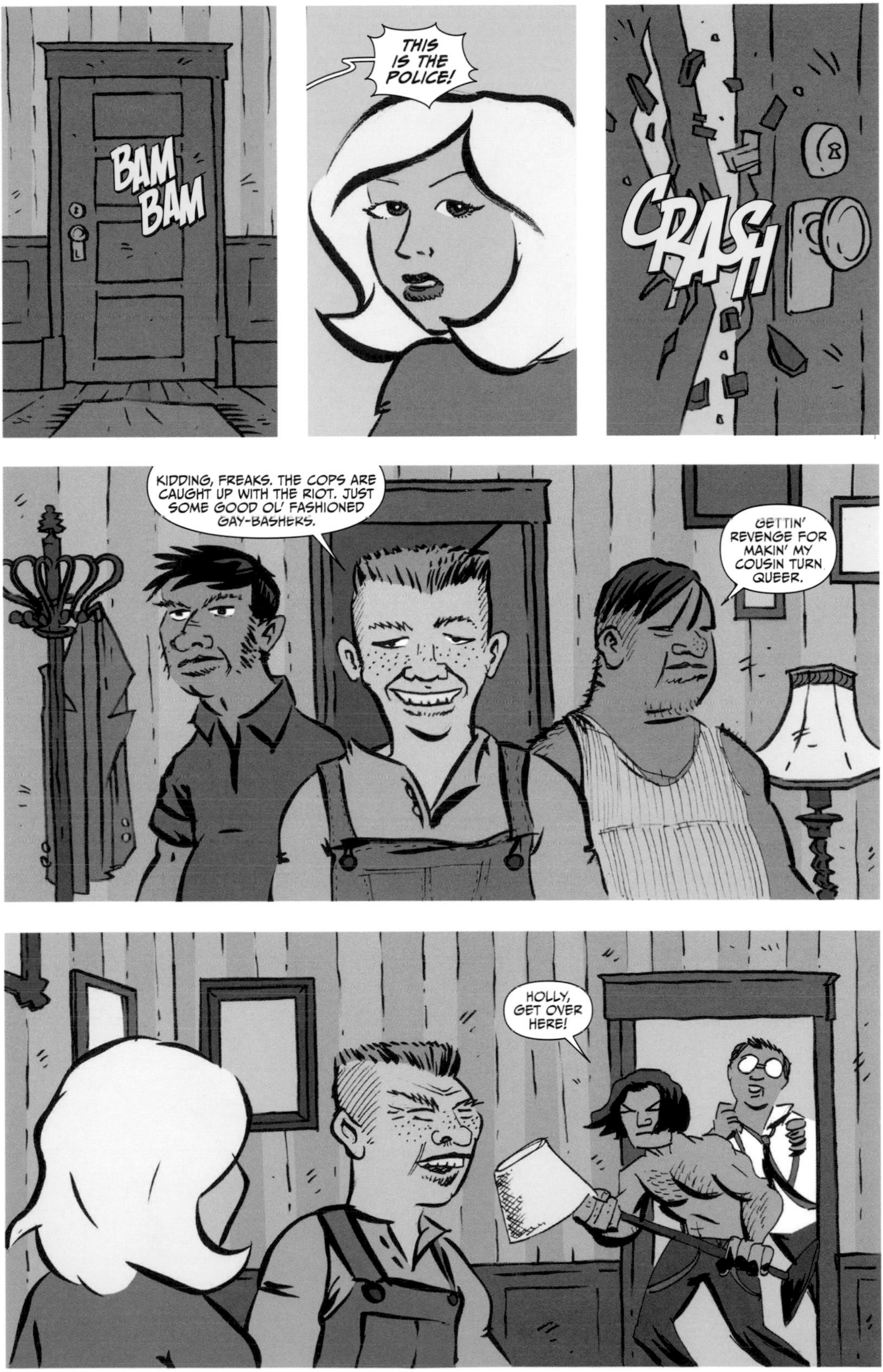
BAM BAM
THIS IS THE POLICE!
CRASH
KIDDING, FREAKS. THE COPS ARE CAUGHT UP WITH THE RIOT. JUST SOME GOOD OL' FASHIONED GAY-BASHERS.
GETTIN' REVENGE FOR MAKIN' MY COUSIN TURN QUEER.
HOLLY, GET OVER HERE!

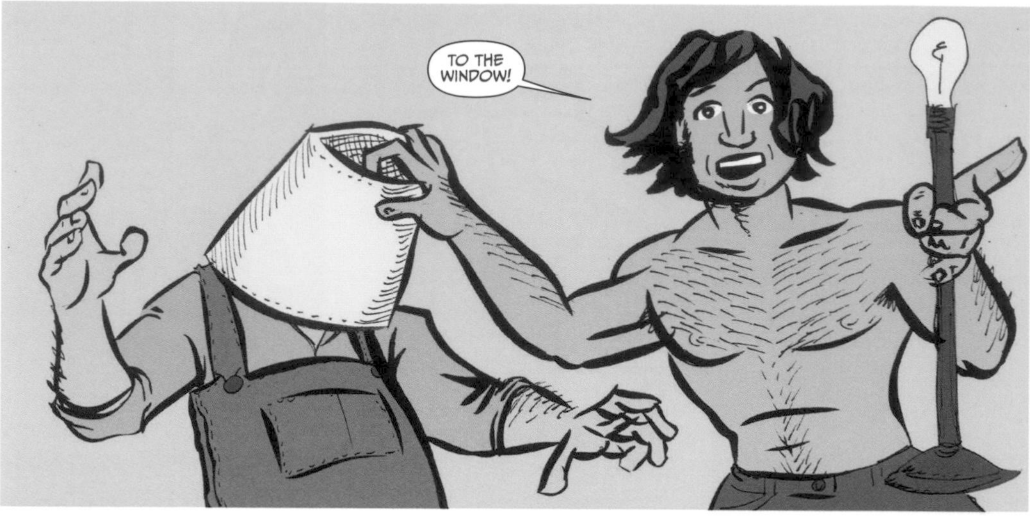
TO THE WINDOW!

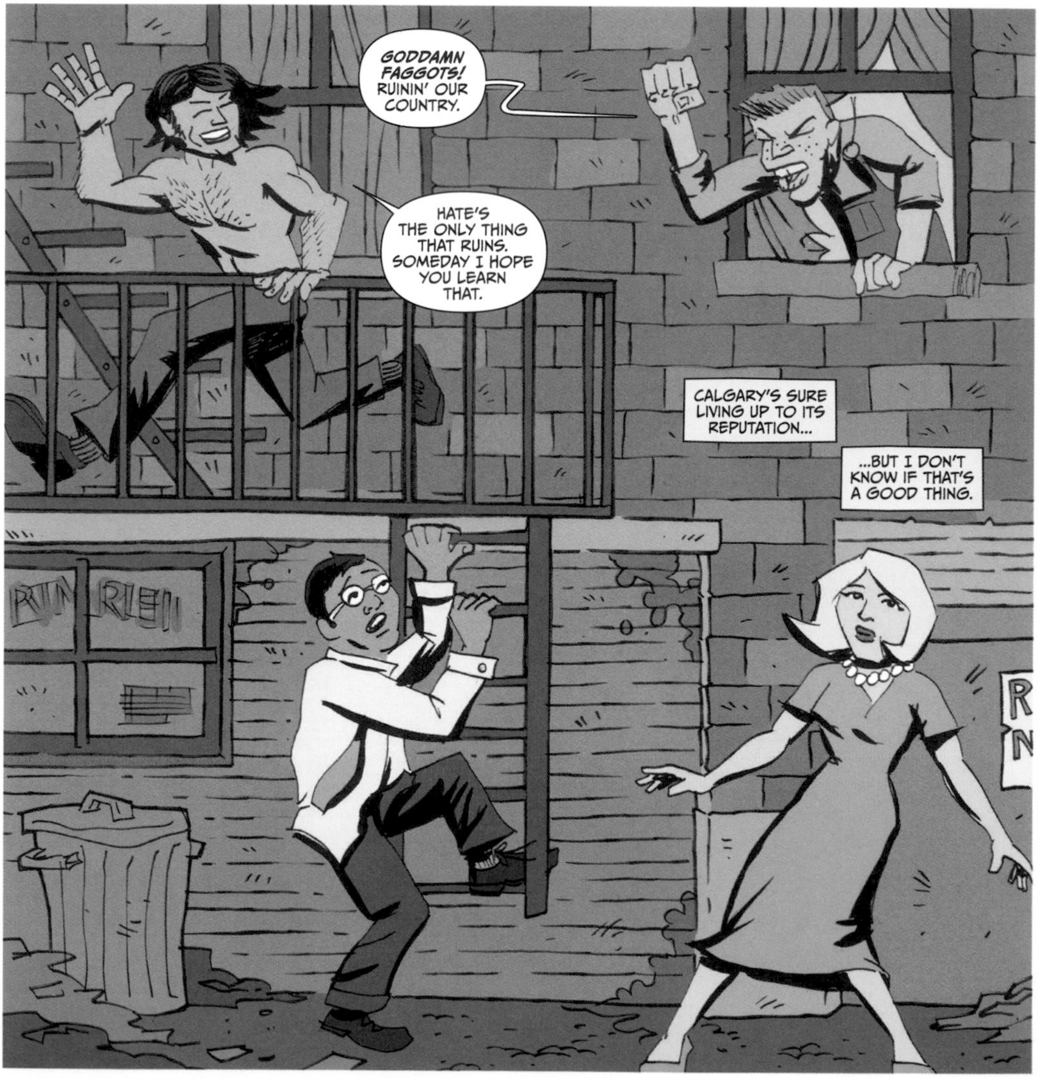
GODDAMN FAGGOTS! RUININ' OUR COUNTRY.
HATE'S THE ONLY THING THAT RUINS. SOMEDAY I HOPE YOU LEARN THAT.
CALGARY'S SURE LIVING UP TO ITS REPUTATION...
...BUT I DON'T KNOW IF THAT'S A GOOD THING.

PART II
WHAT WEALTH COULD MEAN

"The trouble with socialism is that it takes up too many evenings."

- Oscar Wilde

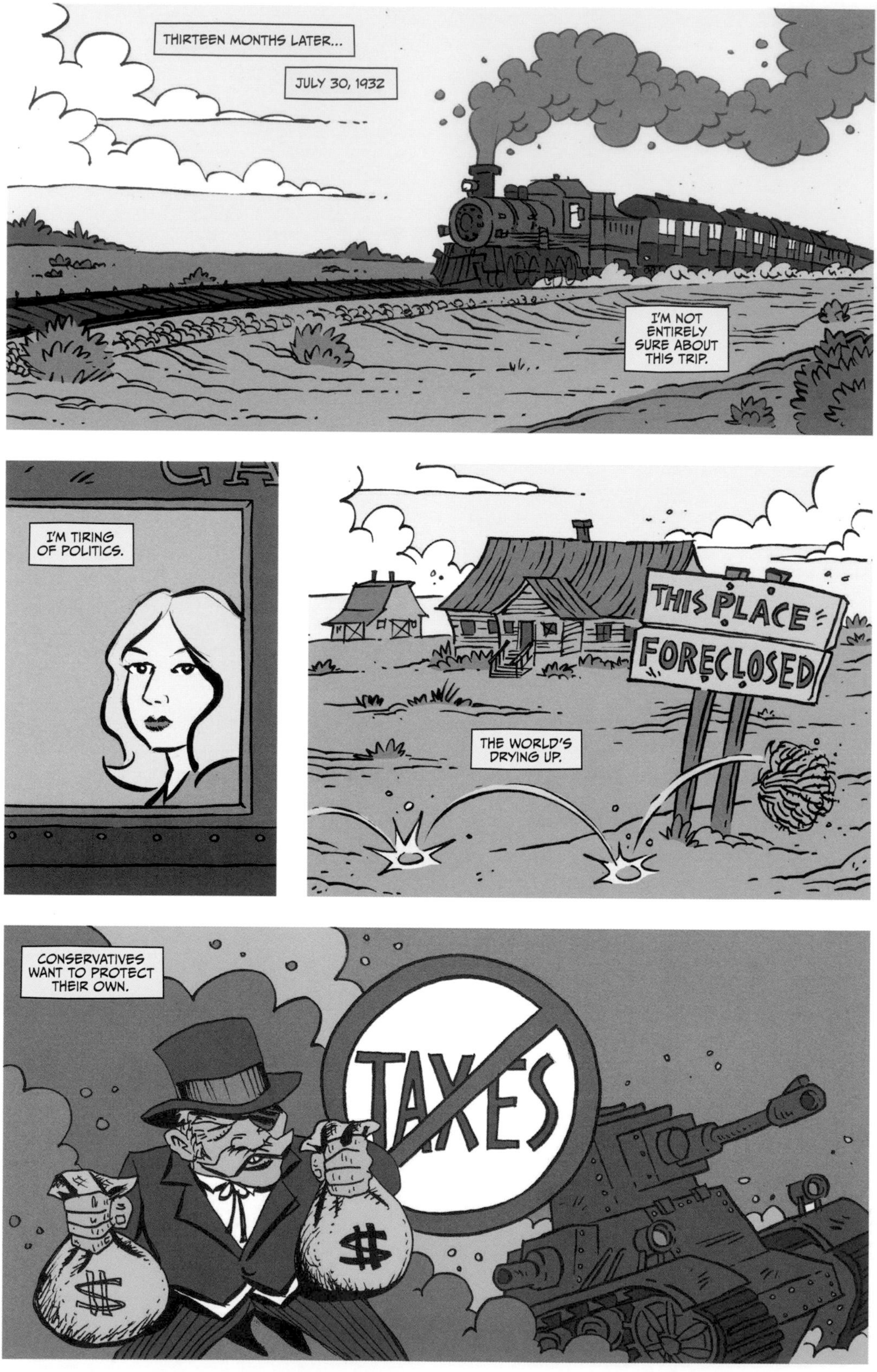
THIRTEEN MONTHS LATER...
JULY 30, 1932
I'M NOT ENTIRELY SURE ABOUT THIS TRIP.
I'M TIRING OF POLITICS.
THIS PLACE FORECLOSED
THE WORLD'S DRYING UP.
CONSERVATIVES WANT TO PROTECT THEIR OWN.
TAXES

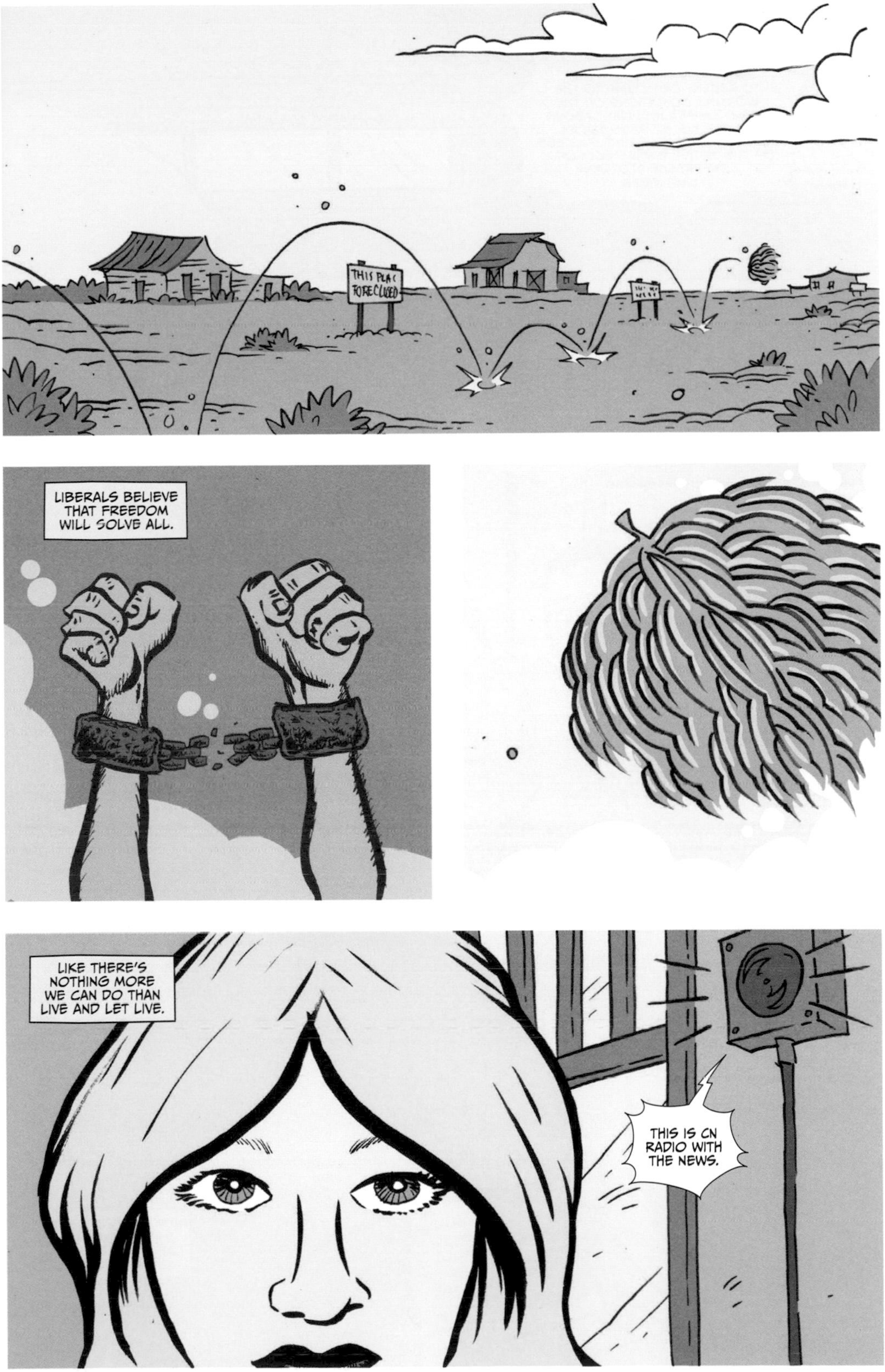

THIS PLAC FORECLOSED
LIBERALS BELIEVE THAT FREEDOM WILL SOLVE ALL.
LIKE THERE'S NOTHING MORE WE CAN DO THAN LIVE AND LET LIVE.
THIS IS CN RADIO WITH THE NEWS.

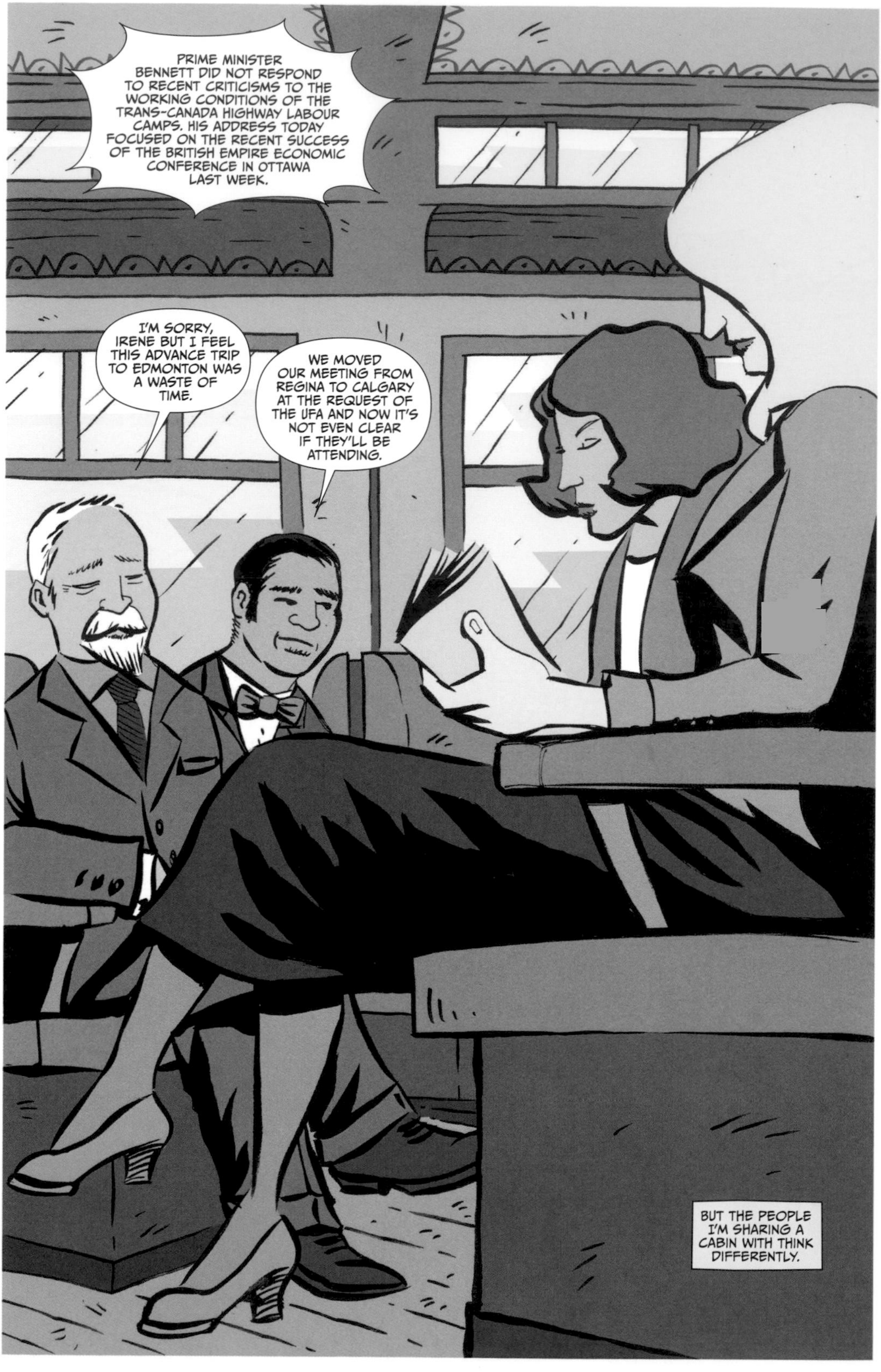
PRIME MINISTER BENNETT DID NOT RESPOND TO RECENT CRITICISMS TO THE WORKING CONDITIONS OF THE TRANS-CANADA HIGHWAY LABOUR CAMPS. HIS ADDRESS TODAY FOCUSED ON THE RECENT SUCCESS OF THE BRITISH EMPIRE ECONOMIC CONFERENCE IN OTTAWA LAST WEEK.
I'M SORRY, IRENE BUT I FEEL THIS ADVANCE TRIP TO EDMONTON WAS A WASTE OF TIME.
WE MOVED OUR MEETING FROM REGINA TO CALGARY AT THE REQUEST OF THE UFA AND NOW IT'S NOT EVEN CLEAR IF THEY'LL BE ATTENDING.
BUT THE PEOPLE I'M SHARING A CABIN WITH THINK DIFFERENTLY.

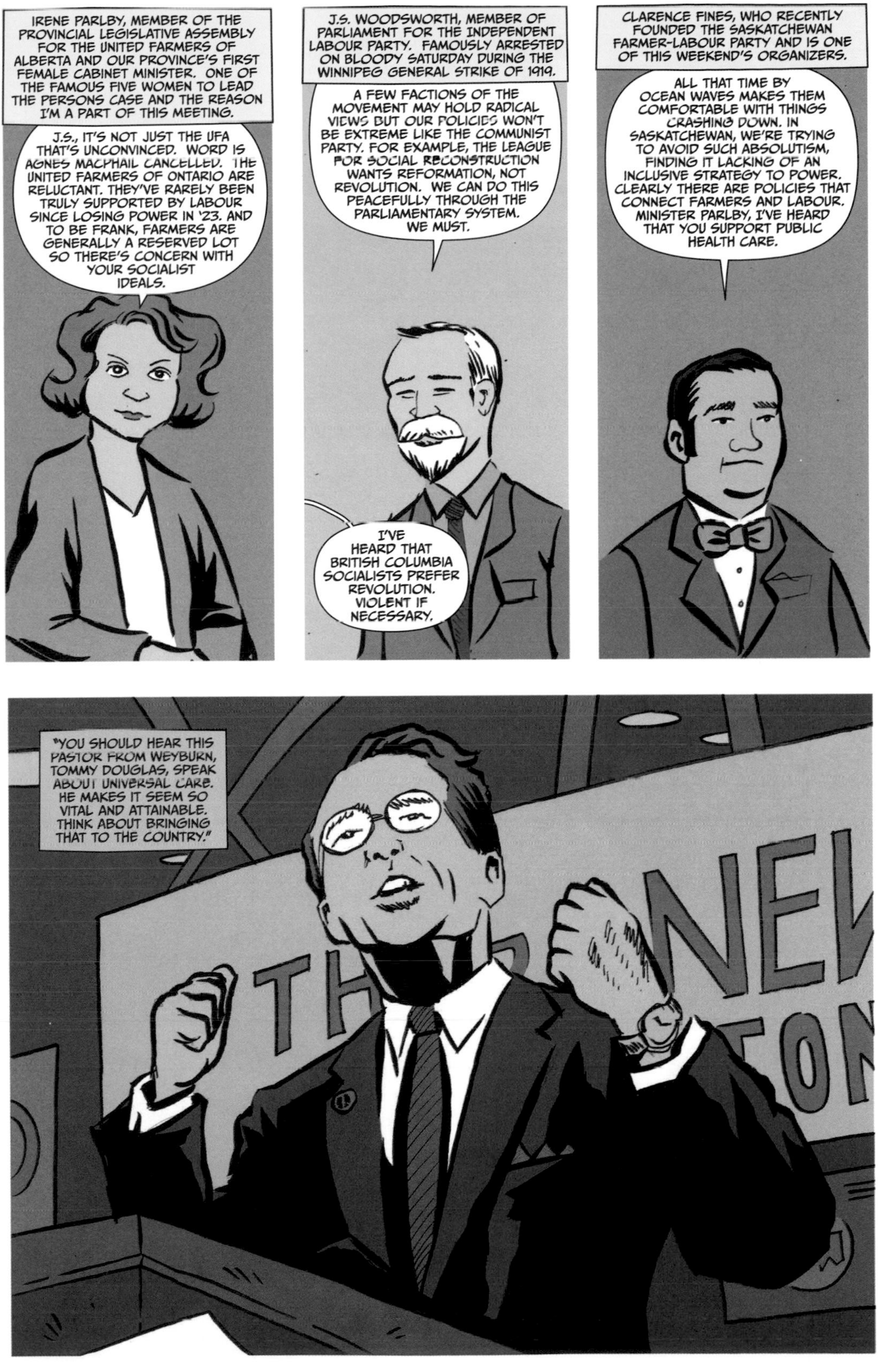
IRENE PARLBY, MEMBER OF THE PROVINCIAL LEGISLATIVE ASSEMBLY FOR THE UNITED FARMERS OF ALBERTA AND OUR PROVINCE'S FIRST FEMALE CABINET MINISTER. ONE OF THE FAMOUS FIVE WOMEN TO LEAD THE PERSONS CASE AND THE REASON I'M A PART OF THIS MEETING.
J.S., IT'S NOT JUST THE UFA THAT'S UNCONVINCED. WORD IS AGNES MACPHAIL CANCELLED. THE UNITED FARMERS OF ONTARIO ARE RELUCTANT. THEY'VE RARELY BEEN TRULY SUPPORTED BY LABOUR SINCE LOSING POWER IN '23. AND TO BE FRANK, FARMERS ARE GENERALLY A RESERVED LOT SO THERE'S CONCERN WITH YOUR SOCIALIST IDEALS.
J.S. WOODSWORTH, MEMBER OF PARLIAMENT FOR THE INDEPENDENT LABOUR PARTY. FAMOUSLY ARRESTED ON BLOODY SATURDAY DURING THE WINNIPEG GENERAL STRIKE OF 1919.
A FEW FACTIONS OF THE MOVEMENT MAY HOLD RADICAL VIEWS BUT OUR POLICIES WON'T BE EXTREME LIKE THE COMMUNIST PARTY. FOR EXAMPLE, THE LEAGUE FOR SOCIAL RECONSTRUCTION WANTS REFORMATION, NOT REVOLUTION. WE CAN DO THIS PEACEFULLY THROUGH THE PARLIAMENTARY SYSTEM. WE MUST.
I'VE HEARD THAT BRITISH COLUMBIA SOCIALISTS PREFER REVOLUTION. VIOLENT IF NECESSARY.
CLARENCE FINES, WHO RECENTLY FOUNDED THE SASKATCHEWAN FARMER-LABOUR PARTY AND IS ONE OF THIS WEEKEND'S ORGANIZERS.
ALL THAT TIME BY OCEAN WAVES MAKES THEM COMFORTABLE WITH THINGS CRASHING DOWN. IN SASKATCHEWAN, WE'RE TRYING TO AVOID SUCH ABSOLUTISM, FINDING IT LACKING OF AN INCLUSIVE STRATEGY TO POWER. CLEARLY THERE ARE POLICIES THAT CONNECT FARMERS AND LABOUR. MINISTER PARLBY, I'VE HEARD THAT YOU SUPPORT PUBLIC HEALTH CARE.
"YOU SHOULD HEAR THIS PASTOR FROM WEYBURN, TOMMY DOUGLAS, SPEAK ABOUT UNIVERSAL CARE. HE MAKES IT SEEM SO VITAL AND ATTAINABLE. THINK ABOUT BRINGING THAT TO THE COUNTRY."

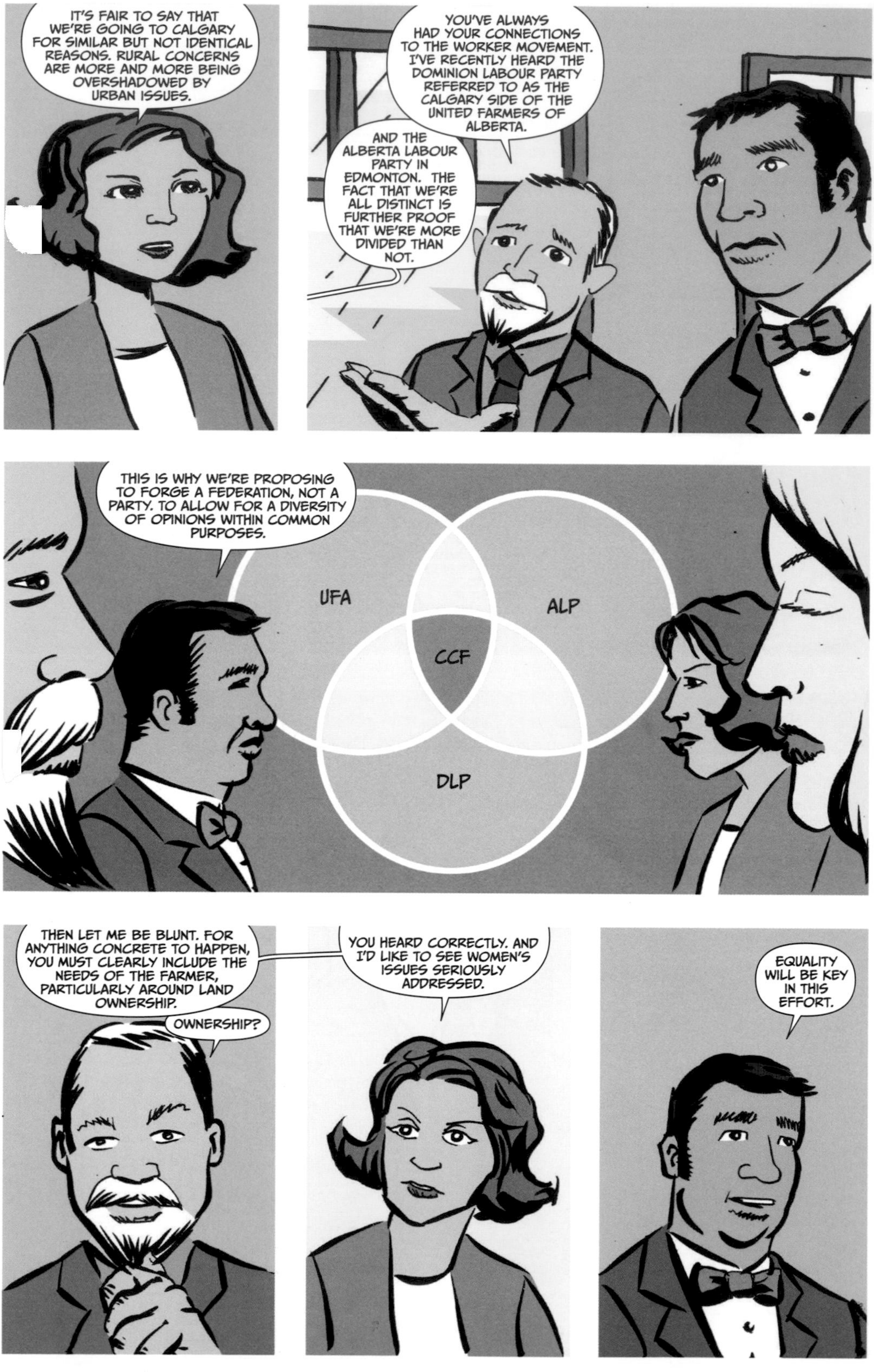
IT'S FAIR TO SAY THAT WE'RE GOING TO CALGARY FOR SIMILAR BUT NOT IDENTICAL REASONS. RURAL CONCERNS ARE MORE AND MORE BEING OVERSHADOWED BY URBAN ISSUES.
YOU'VE ALWAYS HAD YOUR CONNECTIONS TO THE WORKER MOVEMENT. I'VE RECENTLY HEARD THE DOMINION LABOUR PARTY REFERRED TO AS THE CALGARY SIDE OF THE UNITED FARMERS OF ALBERTA.
AND THE ALBERTA LABOUR PARTY IN EDMONTON. THE FACT THAT WE'RE ALL DISTINCT IS FURTHER PROOF THAT WE'RE MORE DIVIDED THAN NOT.
THIS IS WHY WE'RE PROPOSING TO FORGE A FEDERATION, NOT A PARTY. TO ALLOW FOR A DIVERSITY OF OPINIONS WITHIN COMMON PURPOSES.
UFA
ALP
CCF
DLP
THEN LET ME BE BLUNT. FOR ANYTHING CONCRETE TO HAPPEN, YOU MUST CLEARLY INCLUDE THE NEEDS OF THE FARMER, PARTICULARLY AROUND LAND OWNERSHIP.
OWNERSHIP?
YOU HEARD CORRECTLY. AND I'D LIKE TO SEE WOMEN'S ISSUES SERIOUSLY ADDRESSED.
EQUALITY WILL BE KEY IN THIS EFFORT.

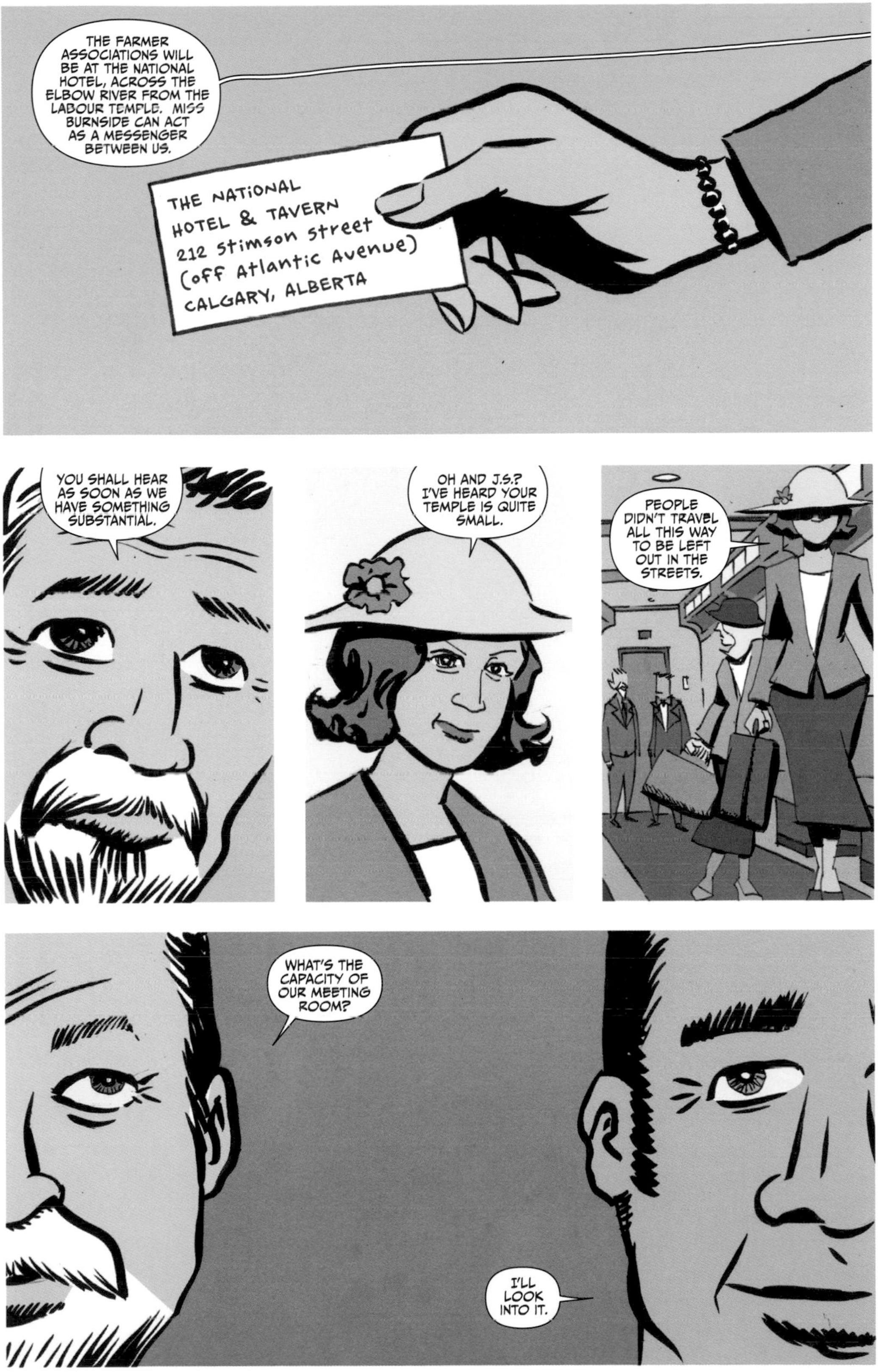
THE FARMER ASSOCIATIONS WILL BE AT THE NATIONAL HOTEL, ACROSS THE ELBOW RIVER FROM THE LABOUR TEMPLE. MISS BURNSIDE CAN ACT AS A MESSENGER BETWEEN US.
THE NATIONAL HOTEL & TAVERN 212 Stimson street (off Atlantic Avenue) CALGARY, ALBERTA
YOU SHALL HEAR AS SOON AS WE HAVE SOMETHING SUBSTANTIAL.
OH AND J.S.? I'VE HEARD YOUR TEMPLE IS QUITE SMALL.
PEOPLE DIDN'T TRAVEL ALL THIS WAY TO BE LEFT OUT IN THE STREETS.
WHAT'S THE CAPACITY OF OUR MEETING ROOM?
I'LL LOOK INTO IT.

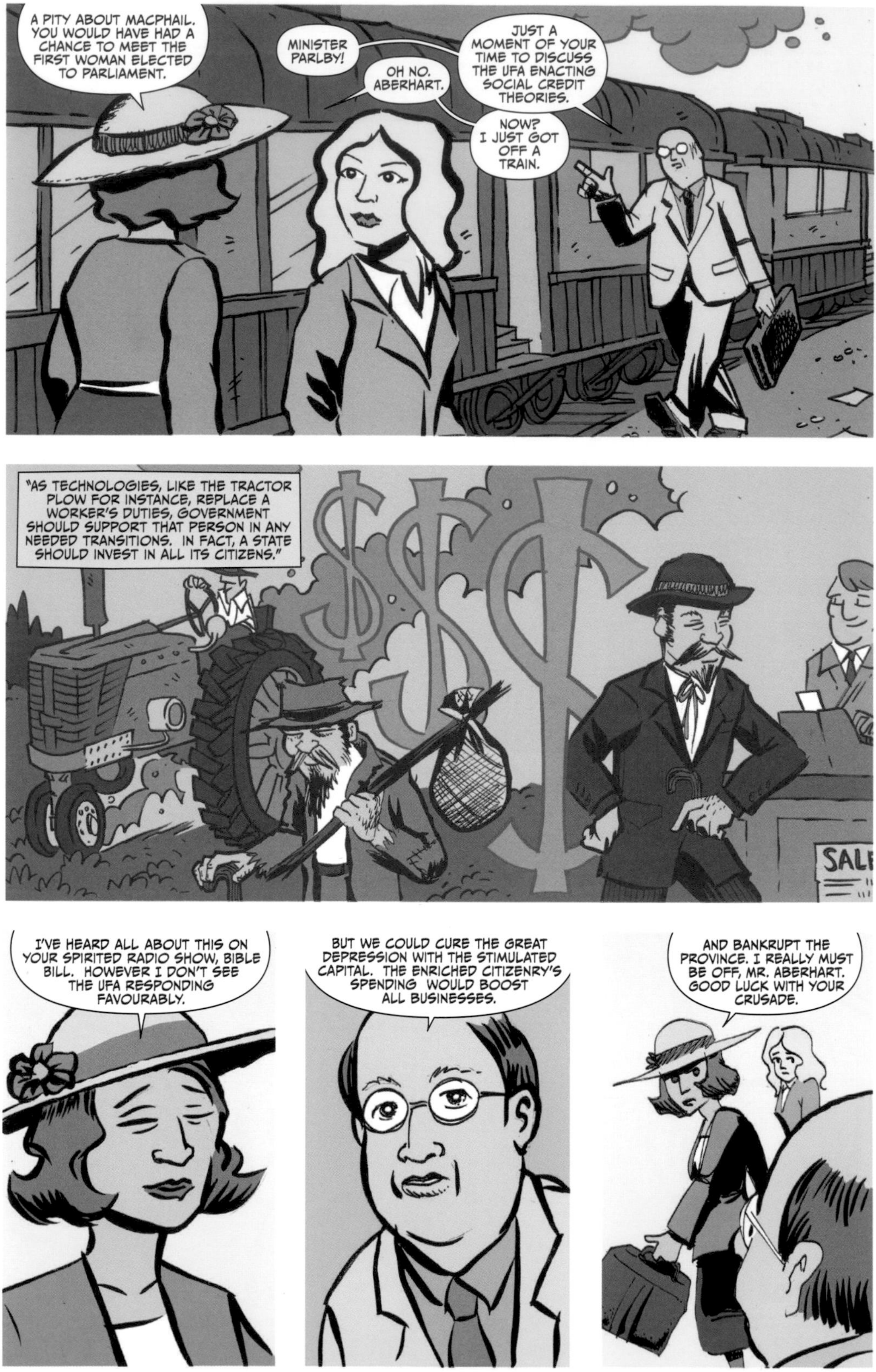
A PITY ABOUT MACPHAIL. YOU WOULD HAVE HAD A CHANCE TO MEET THE FIRST WOMAN ELECTED TO PARLIAMENT.
MINISTER PARLBY!
OH NO. ABERHART.
JUST A MOMENT OF YOUR TIME TO DISCUSS THE UFA ENACTING SOCIAL CREDIT THEORIES.
NOW? I JUST GOT OFF A TRAIN.
"AS TECHNOLOGIES, LIKE THE TRACTOR PLOW FOR INSTANCE, REPLACE A WORKER'S DUTIES, GOVERNMENT SHOULD SUPPORT THAT PERSON IN ANY NEEDED TRANSITIONS. IN FACT, A STATE SHOULD INVEST IN ALL ITS CITIZENS."
SALE
I'VE HEARD ALL ABOUT THIS ON YOUR SPIRITED RADIO SHOW, BIBLE BILL. HOWEVER I DON'T SEE THE UFA RESPONDING FAVOURABLY.
BUT WE COULD CURE THE GREAT DEPRESSION WITH THE STIMULATED CAPITAL. THE ENRICHED CITIZENRY'S SPENDING WOULD BOOST ALL BUSINESSES.
AND BANKRUPT THE PROVINCE. I REALLY MUST BE OFF, MR. ABERHART. GOOD LUCK WITH YOUR CRUSADE.

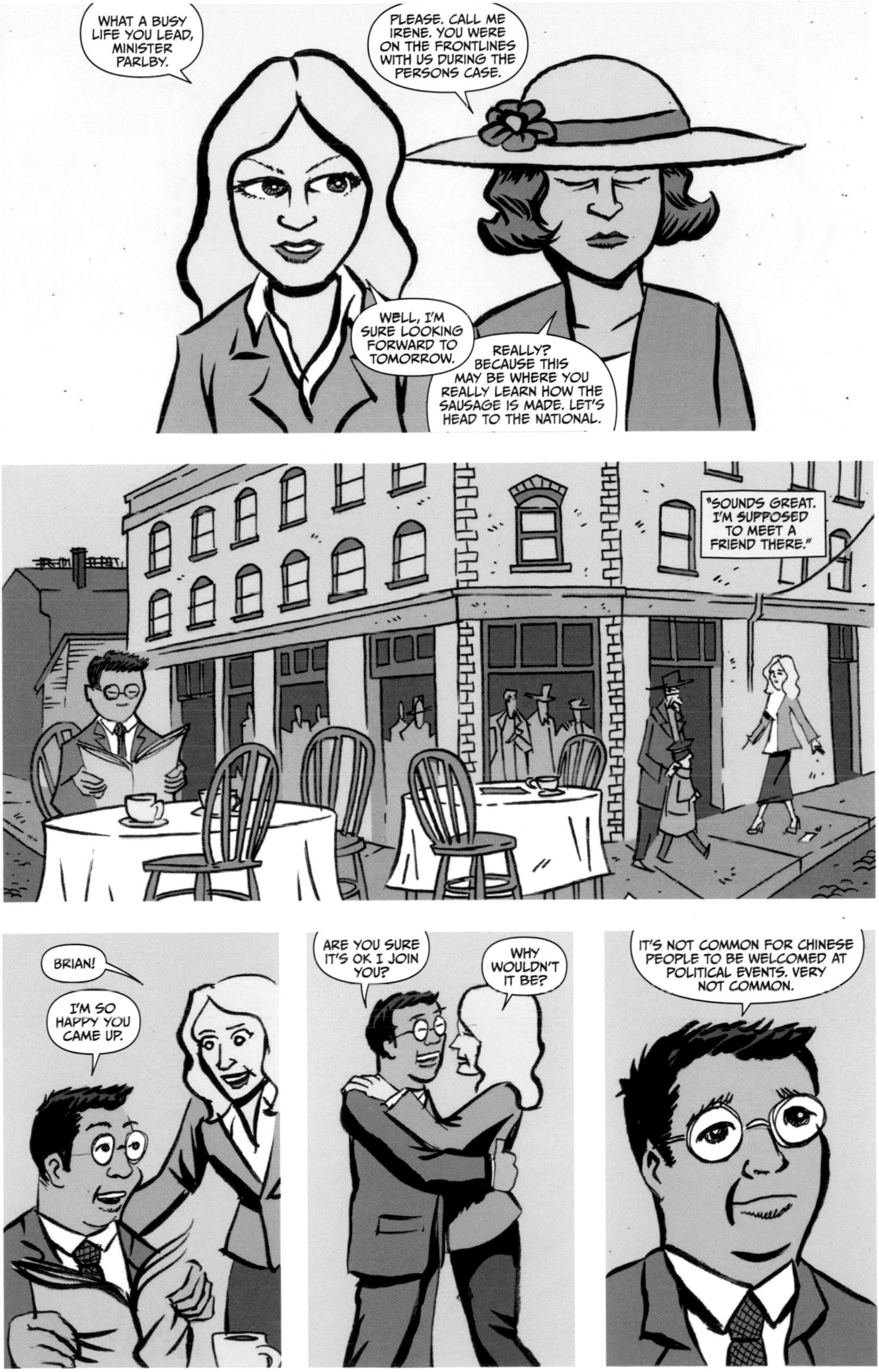
WHAT A BUSY LIFE YOU LEAD, MINISTER PARLBY.
PLEASE. CALL ME IRENE. YOU WERE ON THE FRONTLINES WITH US DURING THE PERSONS CASE.
WELL, I'M SURE LOOKING FORWARD TO TOMORROW.
REALLY? BECAUSE THIS MAY BE WHERE YOU REALLY LEARN HOW THE SAUSAGE IS MADE. LET'S HEAD TO THE NATIONAL.
"SOUNDS GREAT. I'M SUPPOSED TO MEET A FRIEND THERE."
BRIAN!
I'M SO HAPPY YOU CAME UP.
ARE YOU SURE IT'S OK I JOIN YOU?
WHY WOULDN'T IT BE?
IT'S NOT COMMON FOR CHINESE PEOPLE TO BE WELCOMED AT POLITICAL EVENTS. VERY NOT COMMON.

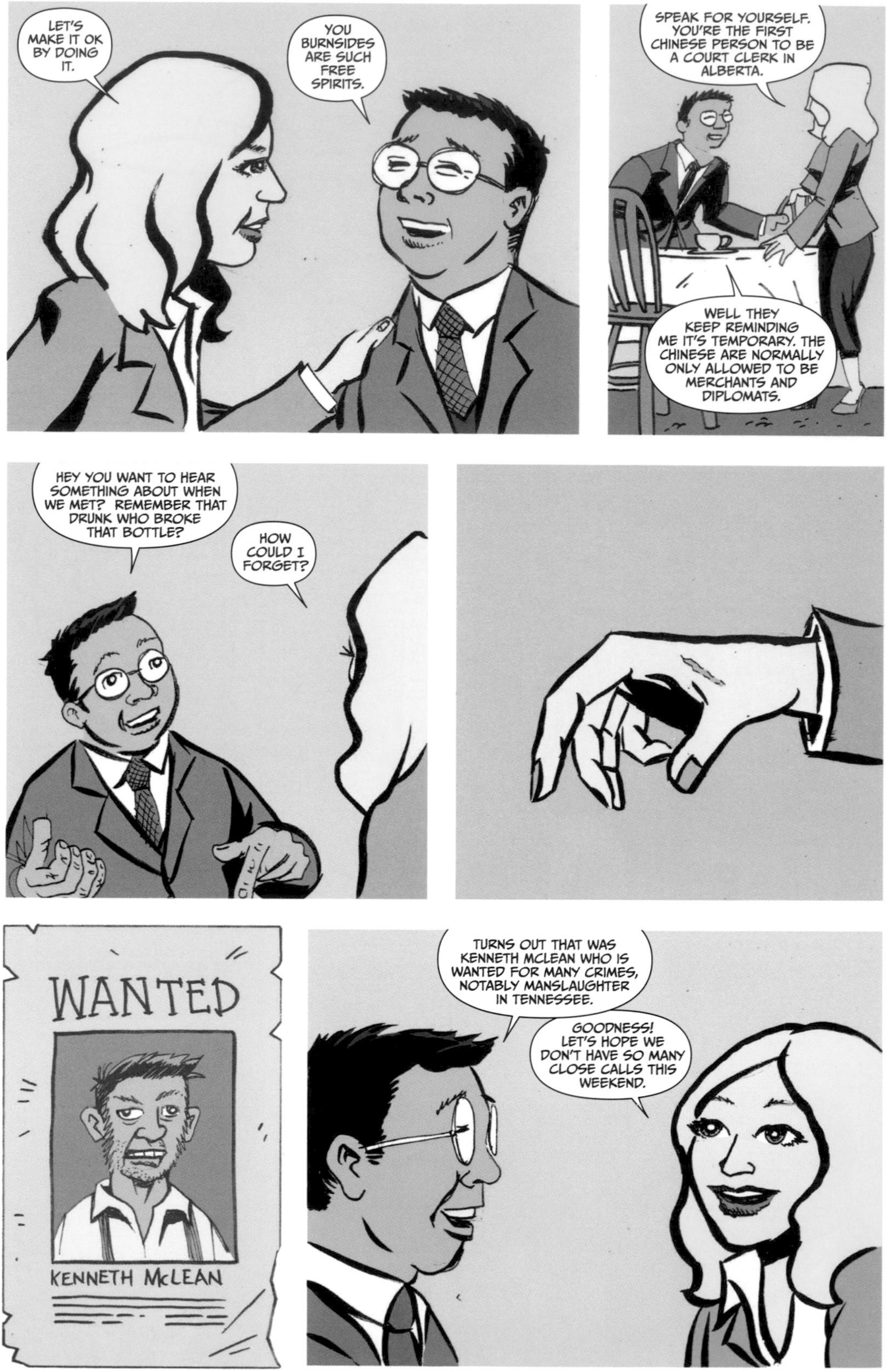
LET'S MAKE IT OK BY DOING IT.
YOU BURNSIDES ARE SUCH FREE SPIRITS.
SPEAK FOR YOURSELF. YOU'RE THE FIRST CHINESE PERSON TO BE A COURT CLERK IN ALBERTA.
WELL THEY KEEP REMINDING ME IT'S TEMPORARY. THE CHINESE ARE NORMALLY ONLY ALLOWED TO BE MERCHANTS AND DIPLOMATS.
HEY YOU WANT TO HEAR SOMETHING ABOUT WHEN WE MET? REMEMBER THAT DRUNK WHO BROKE THAT BOTTLE?
HOW COULD I FORGET?
WANTED
KENNETH McLEAN
TURNS OUT THAT WAS KENNETH MCLEAN WHO IS WANTED FOR MANY CRIMES, NOTABLY MANSLAUGHTER IN TENNESSEE.
GOODNESS! LET'S HOPE WE DON'T HAVE SO MANY CLOSE CALLS THIS WEEKEND.

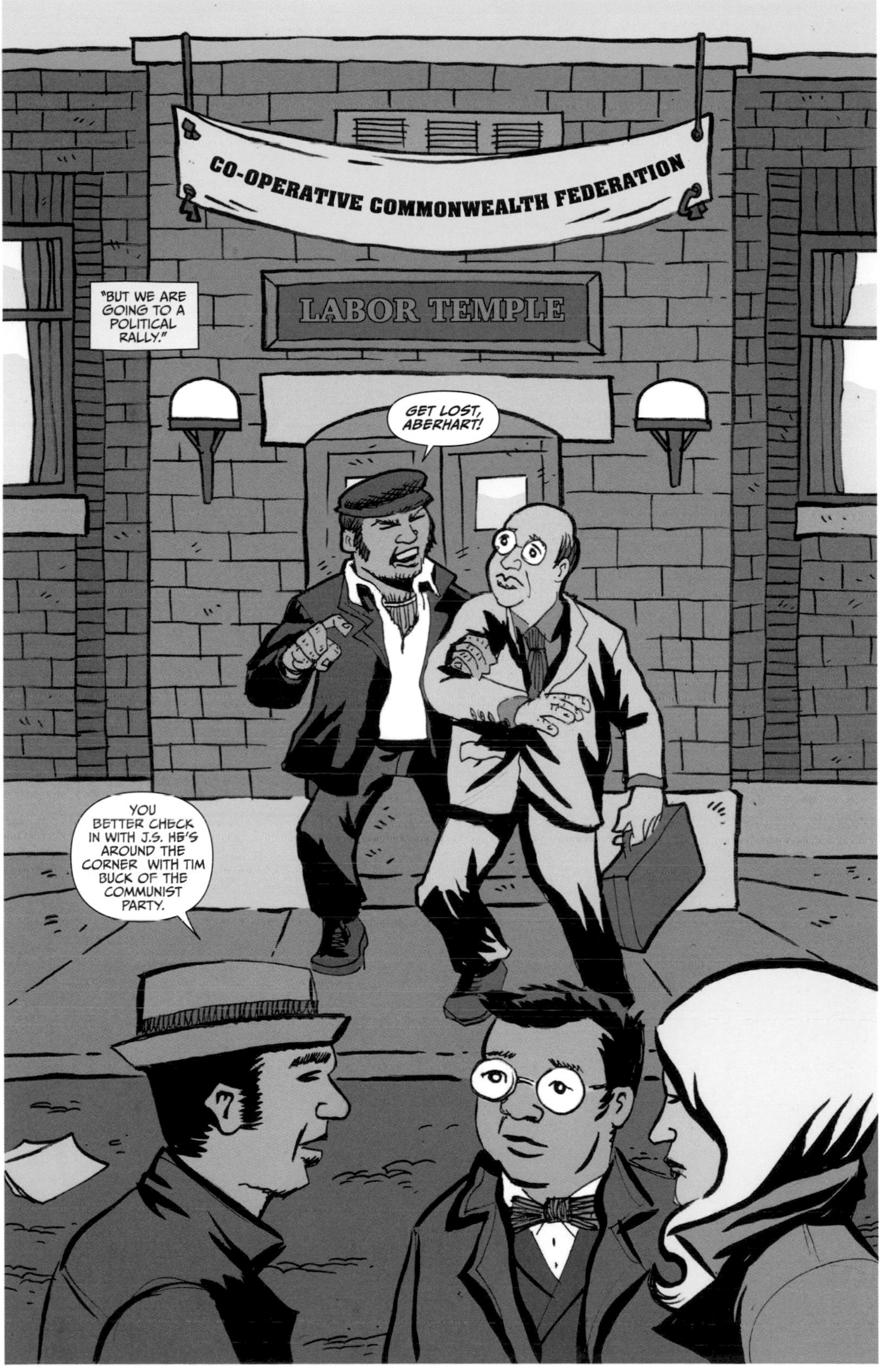

CO-OPERATIVE COMMONWEALTH FEDERATION
LABOR TEMPLE
"BUT WE ARE GOING TO A POLITICAL RALLY."
GET LOST, ABERHART!
YOU BETTER CHECK IN WITH J.S. HE'S AROUND THE CORNER WITH TIM BUCK OF THE COMMUNIST PARTY.

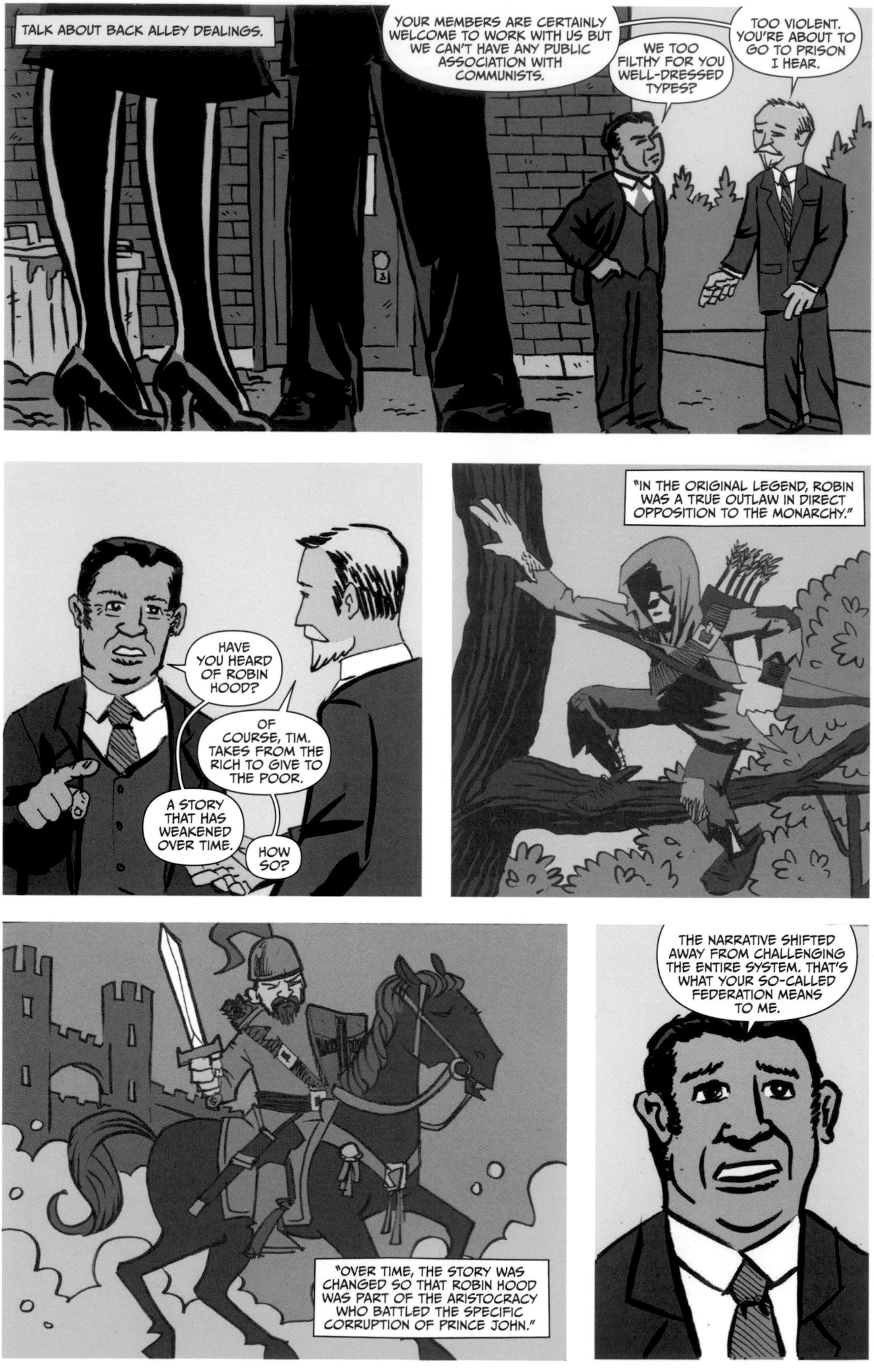
TALK ABOUT BACK ALLEY DEALINGS.
YOUR MEMBERS ARE CERTAINLY WELCOME TO WORK WITH US BUT WE CAN'T HAVE ANY PUBLIC ASSOCIATION WITH COMMUNISTS.
WE TOO FILTHY FOR YOU WELL-DRESSED TYPES?
TOO VIOLENT. YOU'RE ABOUT TO GO TO PRISON I HEAR.
HAVE YOU HEARD OF ROBIN HOOD?
OF COURSE, TIM. TAKES FROM THE RICH TO GIVE TO THE POOR.
A STORY THAT HAS WEAKENED OVER TIME.
HOW SO?
"IN THE ORIGINAL LEGEND, ROBIN WAS A TRUE OUTLAW IN DIRECT OPPOSITION TO THE MONARCHY."
"OVER TIME, THE STORY WAS CHANGED SO THAT ROBIN HOOD WAS PART OF THE ARISTOCRACY WHO BATTLED THE SPECIFIC CORRUPTION OF PRINCE JOHN."
THE NARRATIVE SHIFTED AWAY FROM CHALLENGING THE ENTIRE SYSTEM. THAT'S WHAT YOUR SO-CALLED FEDERATION MEANS TO ME.

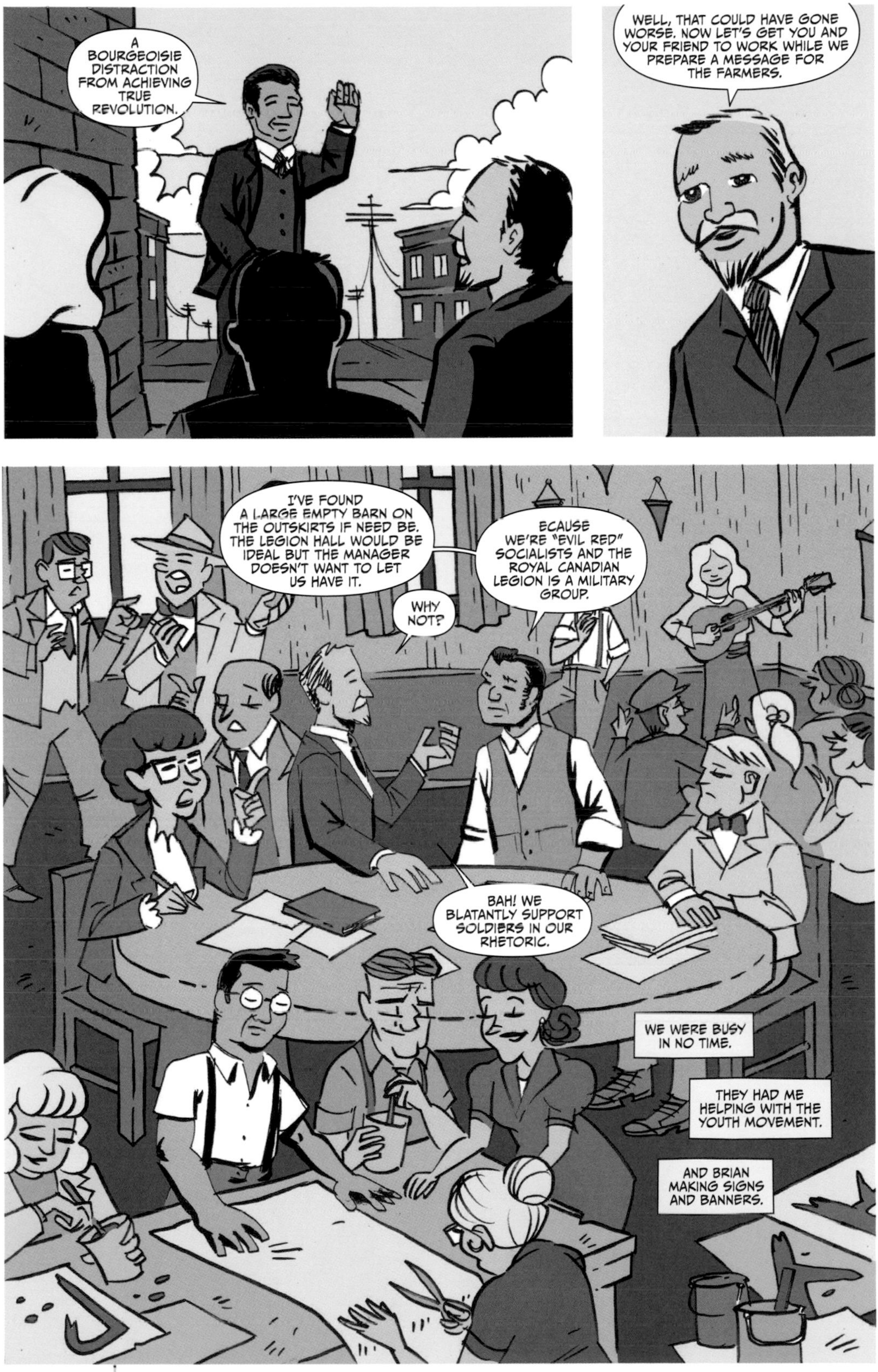

A BOURGEOISIE DISTRACTION FROM ACHIEVING TRUE REVOLUTION.
WELL, THAT COULD HAVE GONE WORSE. NOW LET'S GET YOU AND YOUR FRIEND TO WORK WHILE WE PREPARE A MESSAGE FOR THE FARMERS.
I'VE FOUND A LARGE EMPTY BARN ON THE OUTSKIRTS IF NEED BE. THE LEGION HALL WOULD BE IDEAL BUT THE MANAGER DOESN'T WANT TO LET US HAVE IT.
WHY NOT?
ECAUSE WE'RE "EVIL RED" SOCIALISTS AND THE ROYAL CANADIAN LEGION IS A MILITARY GROUP.
BAH! WE BLATANTLY SUPPORT SOLDIERS IN OUR RHETORIC.
WE WERE BUSY IN NO TIME.
THEY HAD ME HELPING WITH THE YOUTH MOVEMENT.
AND BRIAN MAKING SIGNS AND BANNERS.

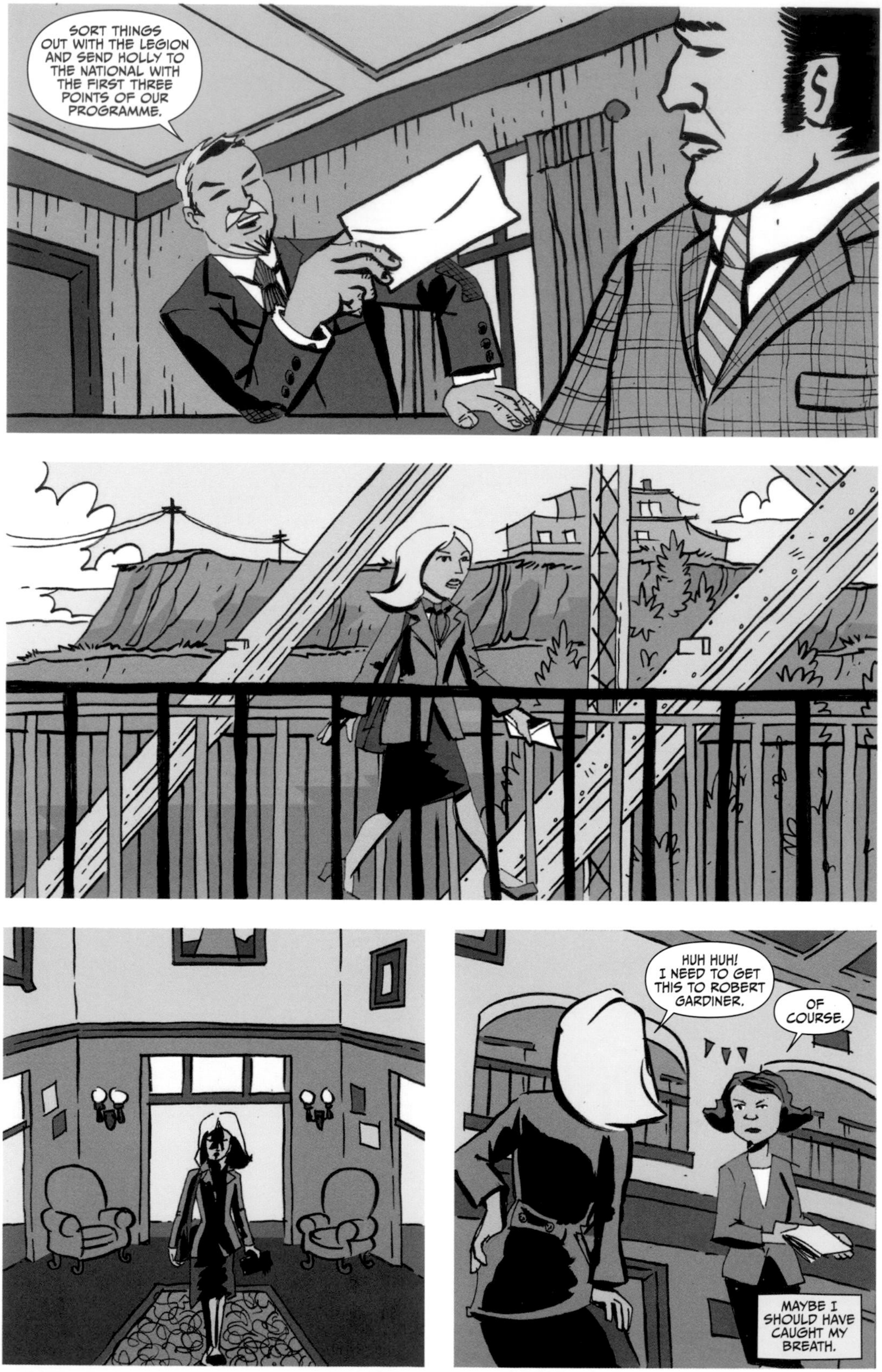
SORT THINGS OUT WITH THE LEGION AND SEND HOLLY TO THE NATIONAL WITH THE FIRST THREE POINTS OF OUR PROGRAMME.
HUH HUH! I NEED TO GET THIS TO ROBERT GARDINER.
OF COURSE.
MAYBE I SHOULD HAVE CAUGHT MY BREATH.

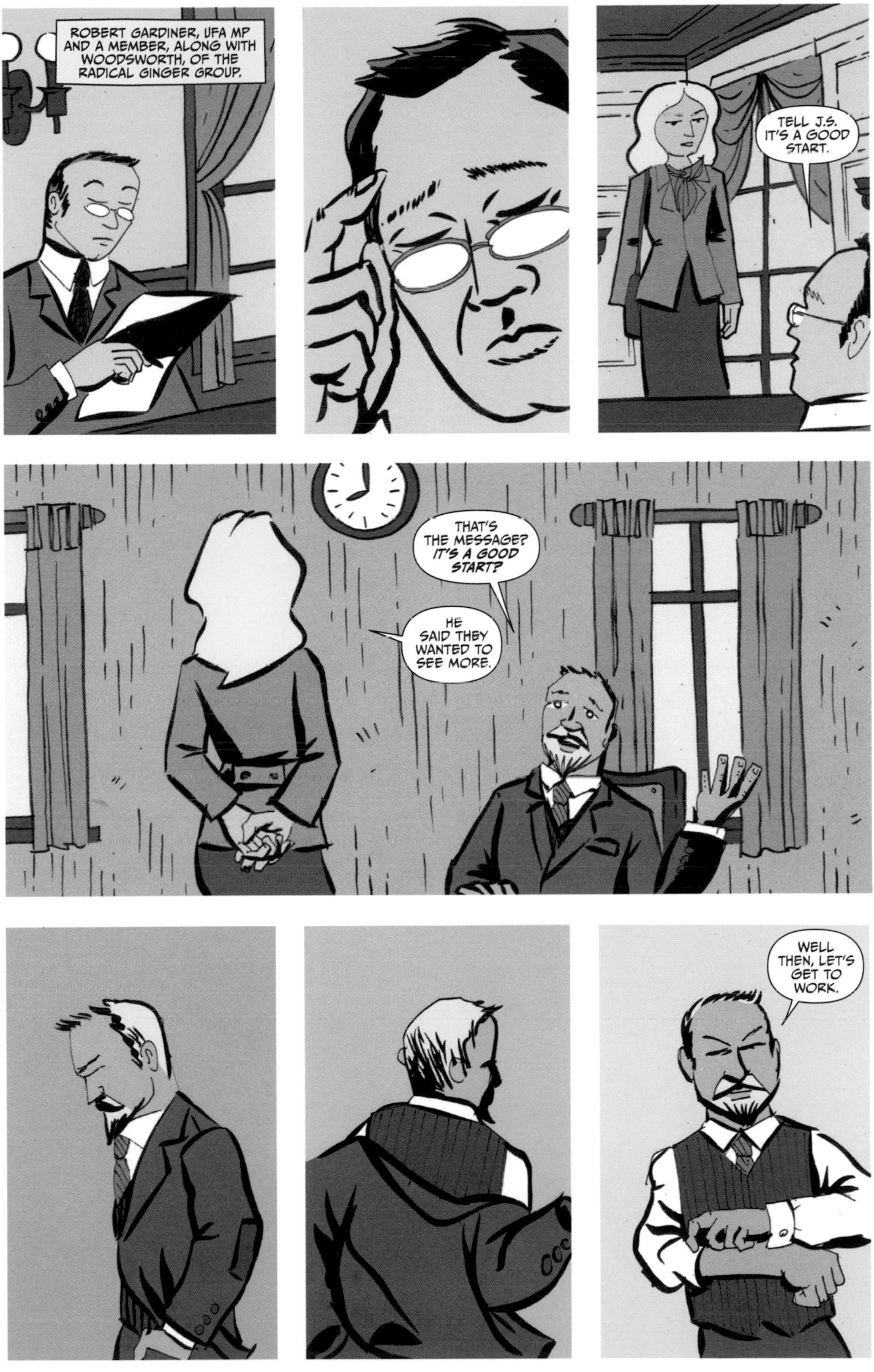
ROBERT GARDINER, UFA MP AND A MEMBER, ALONG WITH WOODSWORTH, OF THE RADICAL GINGER GROUP.
TELL J.S. IT'S A GOOD START.
THAT'S THE MESSAGE? *IT'S A GOOD START?*
HE SAID THEY WANTED TO SEE MORE.
WELL THEN, LET'S GET TO WORK.

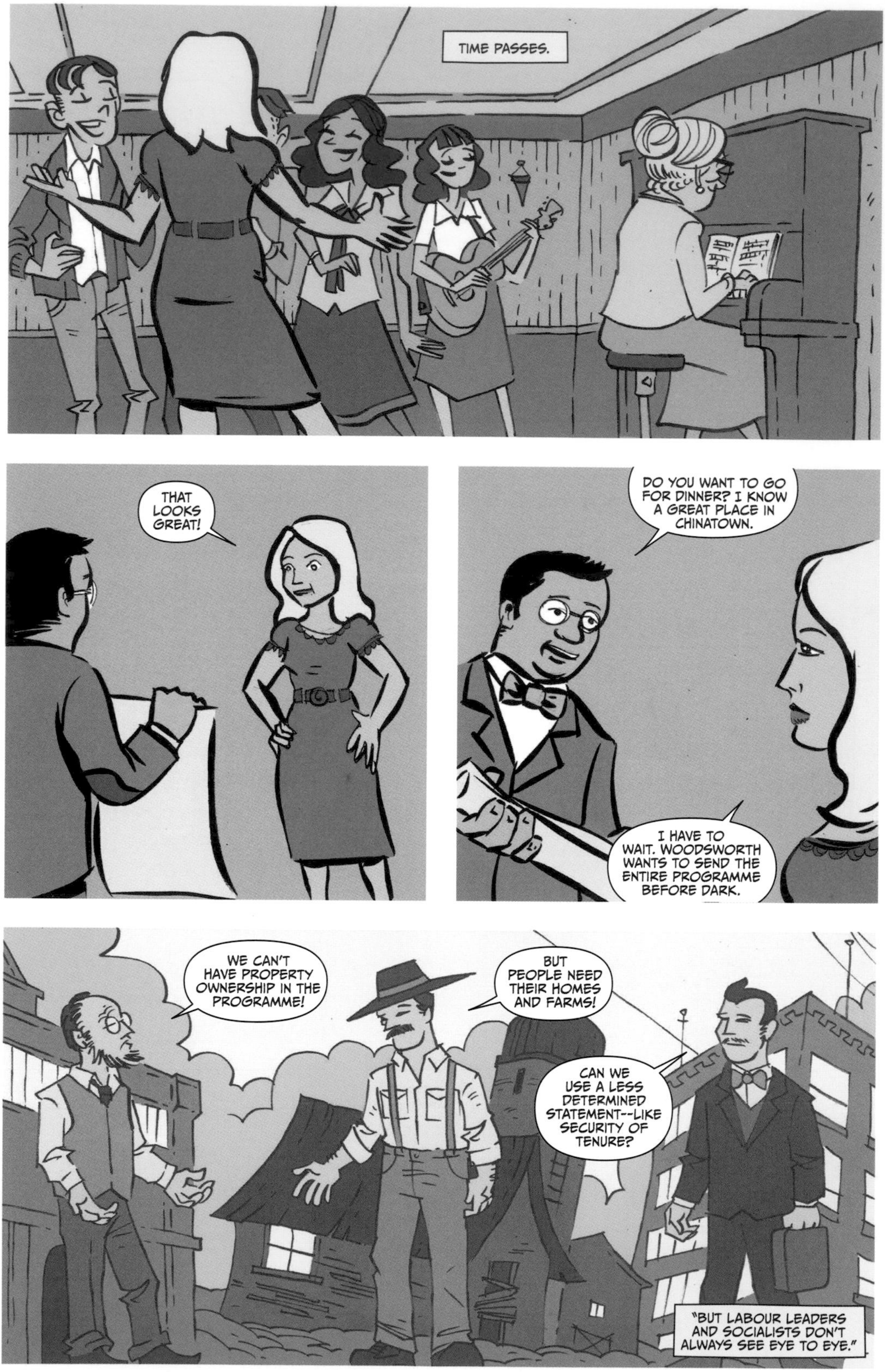
TIME PASSES.
THAT LOOKS GREAT!
DO YOU WANT TO GO FOR DINNER? I KNOW A GREAT PLACE IN CHINATOWN.
I HAVE TO WAIT. WOODSWORTH WANTS TO SEND THE ENTIRE PROGRAMME BEFORE DARK.
WE CAN'T HAVE PROPERTY OWNERSHIP IN THE PROGRAMME!
BUT PEOPLE NEED THEIR HOMES AND FARMS!
CAN WE USE A LESS DETERMINED STATEMENT--LIKE SECURITY OF TENURE?
"BUT LABOUR LEADERS AND SOCIALISTS DON'T ALWAYS SEE EYE TO EYE."

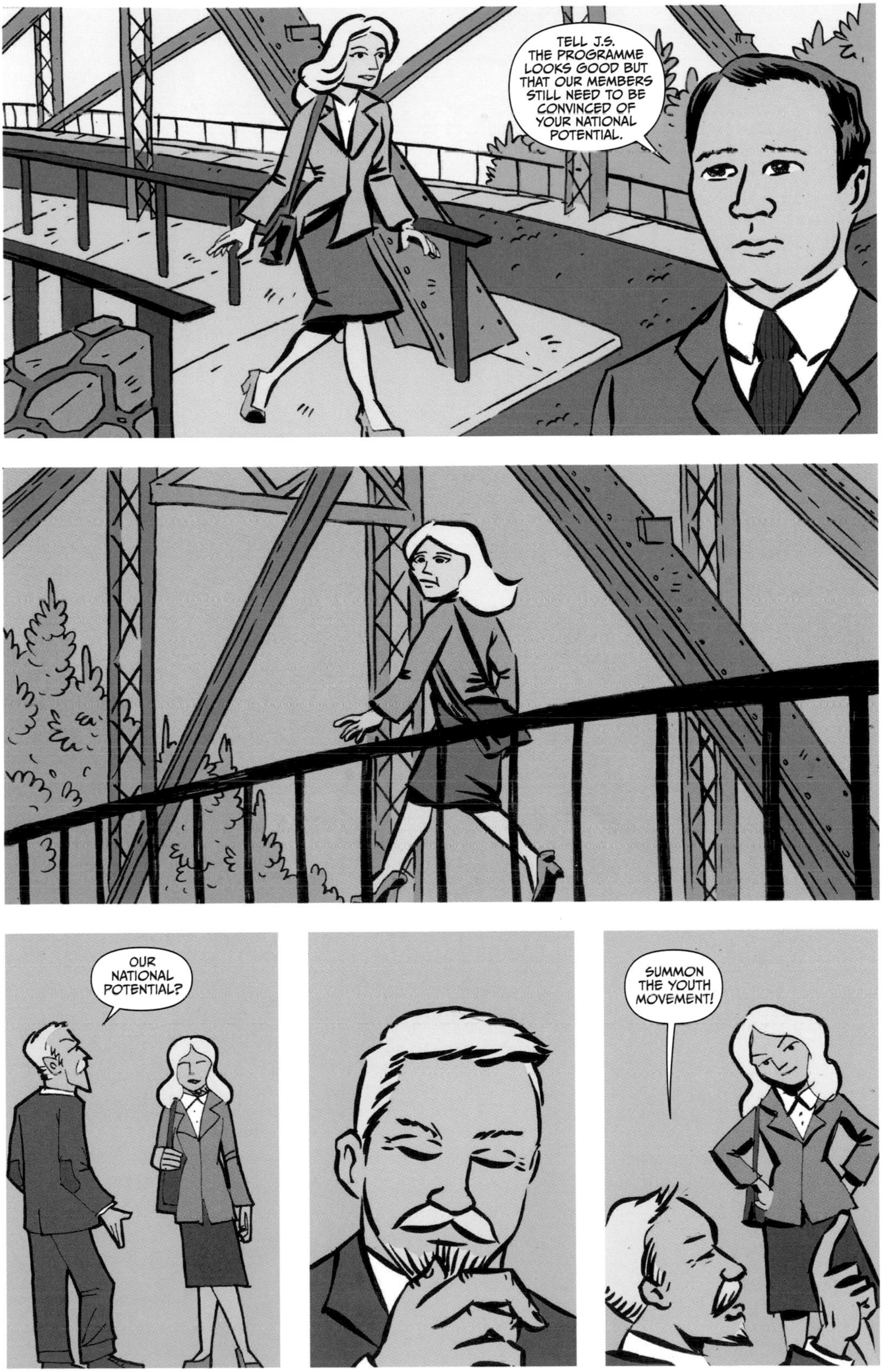
TELL J.S. THE PROGRAMME LOOKS GOOD BUT THAT OUR MEMBERS STILL NEED TO BE CONVINCED OF YOUR NATIONAL POTENTIAL.
OUR NATIONAL POTENTIAL?
SUMMON THE YOUTH MOVEMENT!

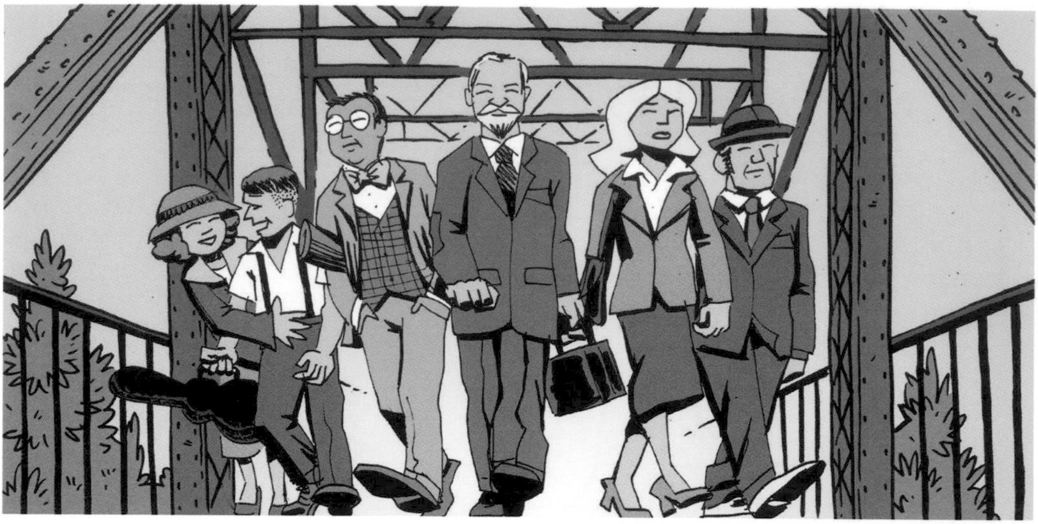

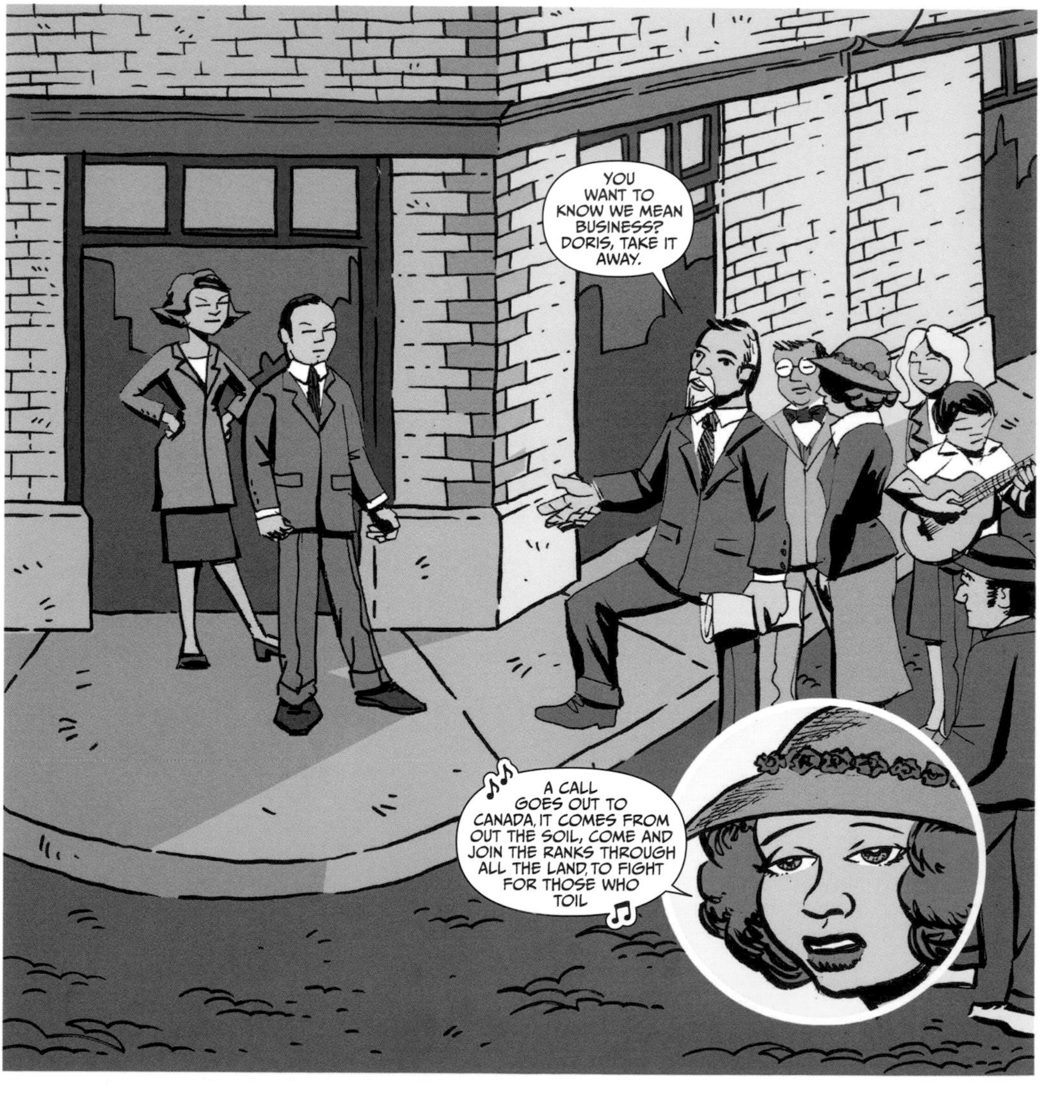
YOU WANT TO KNOW WE MEAN BUSINESS? DORIS, TAKE IT AWAY.
A CALL GOES OUT TO CANADA, IT COMES FROM OUT THE SOIL, COME AND JOIN THE RANKS THROUGH ALL THE LAND, TO FIGHT FOR THOSE WHO TOIL

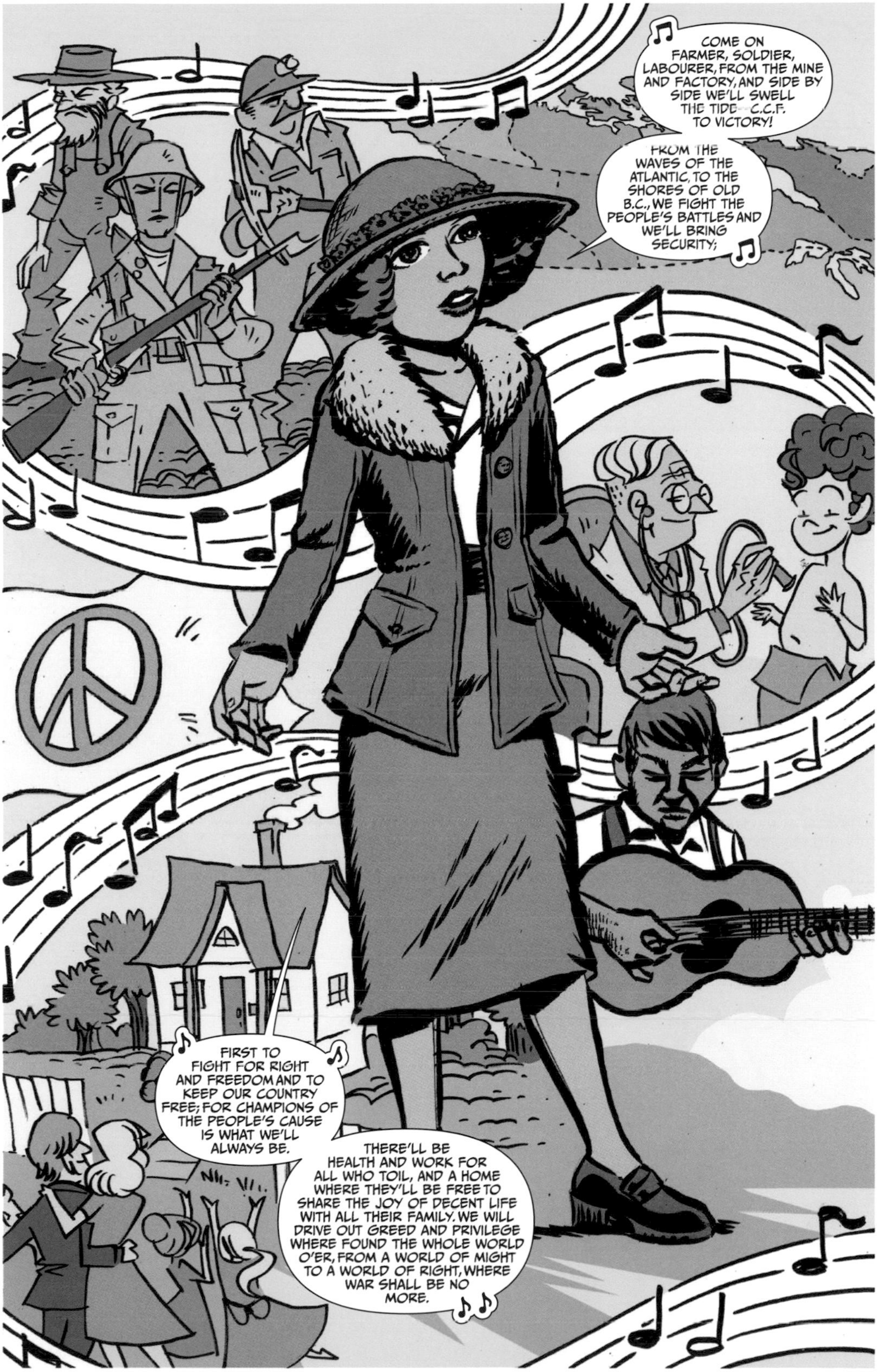
COME ON FARMER, SOLDIER, LABOURER, FROM THE MINE AND FACTORY, AND SIDE BY SIDE WE'LL SWELL THE TIDE– C.C.F. TO VICTORY!
FROM THE WAVES OF THE ATLANTIC, TO THE SHORES OF OLD B.C., WE FIGHT THE PEOPLE'S BATTLES AND WE'LL BRING SECURITY;
FIRST TO FIGHT FOR RIGHT AND FREEDOM AND TO KEEP OUR COUNTRY FREE; FOR CHAMPIONS OF THE PEOPLE'S CAUSE IS WHAT WE'LL ALWAYS BE.
THERE'LL BE HEALTH AND WORK FOR ALL WHO TOIL, AND A HOME WHERE THEY'LL BE FREE TO SHARE THE JOY OF DECENT LIFE WITH ALL THEIR FAMILY. WE WILL DRIVE OUT GREED AND PRIVILEGE WHERE FOUND THE WHOLE WORLD O'ER, FROM A WORLD OF MIGHT TO A WORLD OF RIGHT, WHERE WAR SHALL BE NO MORE.

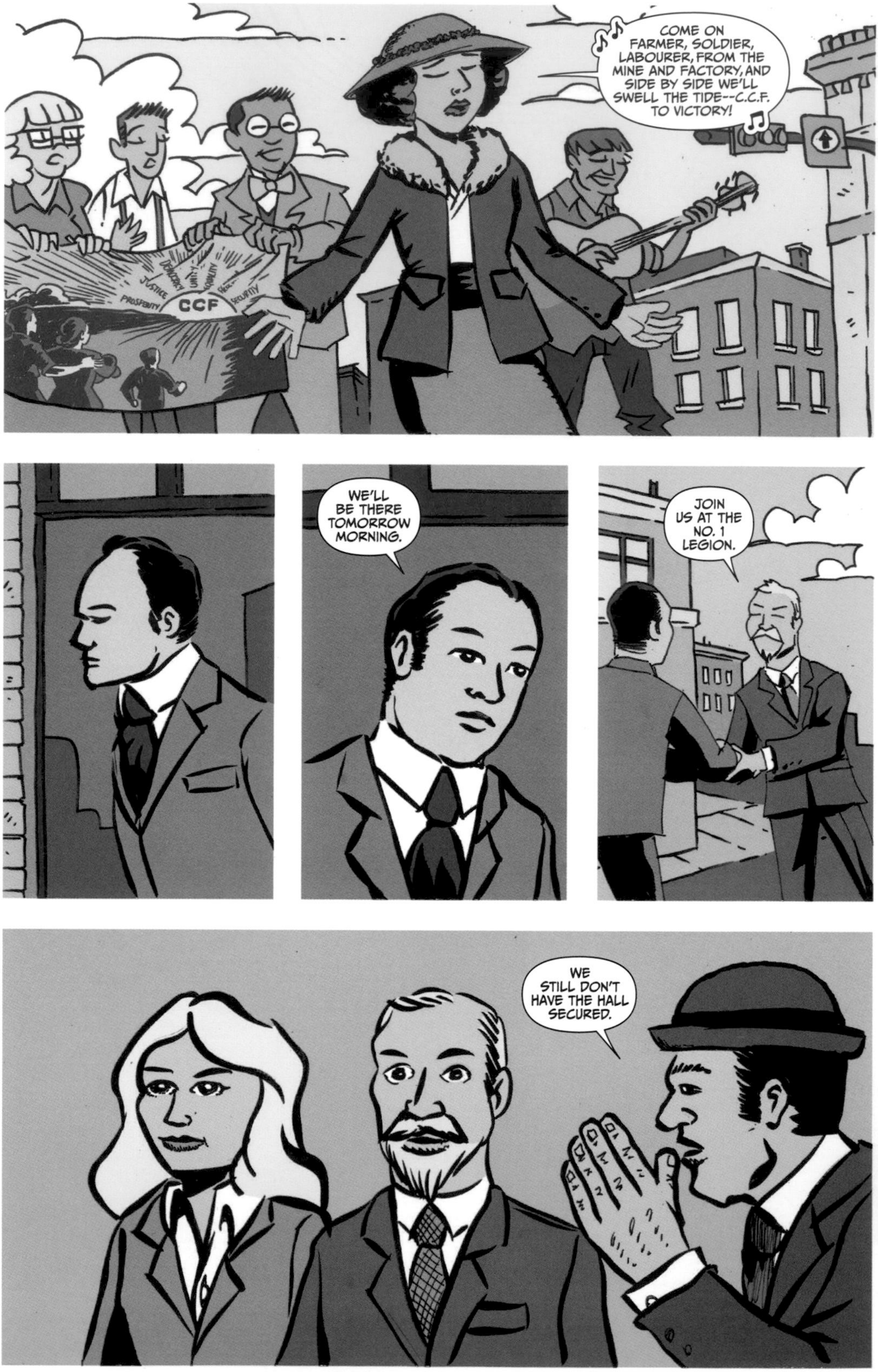
COME ON FARMER, SOLDIER, LABOURER, FROM THE MINE AND FACTORY, AND SIDE BY SIDE WE'LL SWELL THE TIDE--C.C.F. TO VICTORY!
PROSPERITY
JUSTICE
DEMOCRACY
UNITY
EQUALITY
SECURITY
CCF
WE'LL BE THERE TOMORROW MORNING.
JOIN US AT THE NO. 1 LEGION.
WE STILL DON'T HAVE THE HALL SECURED.

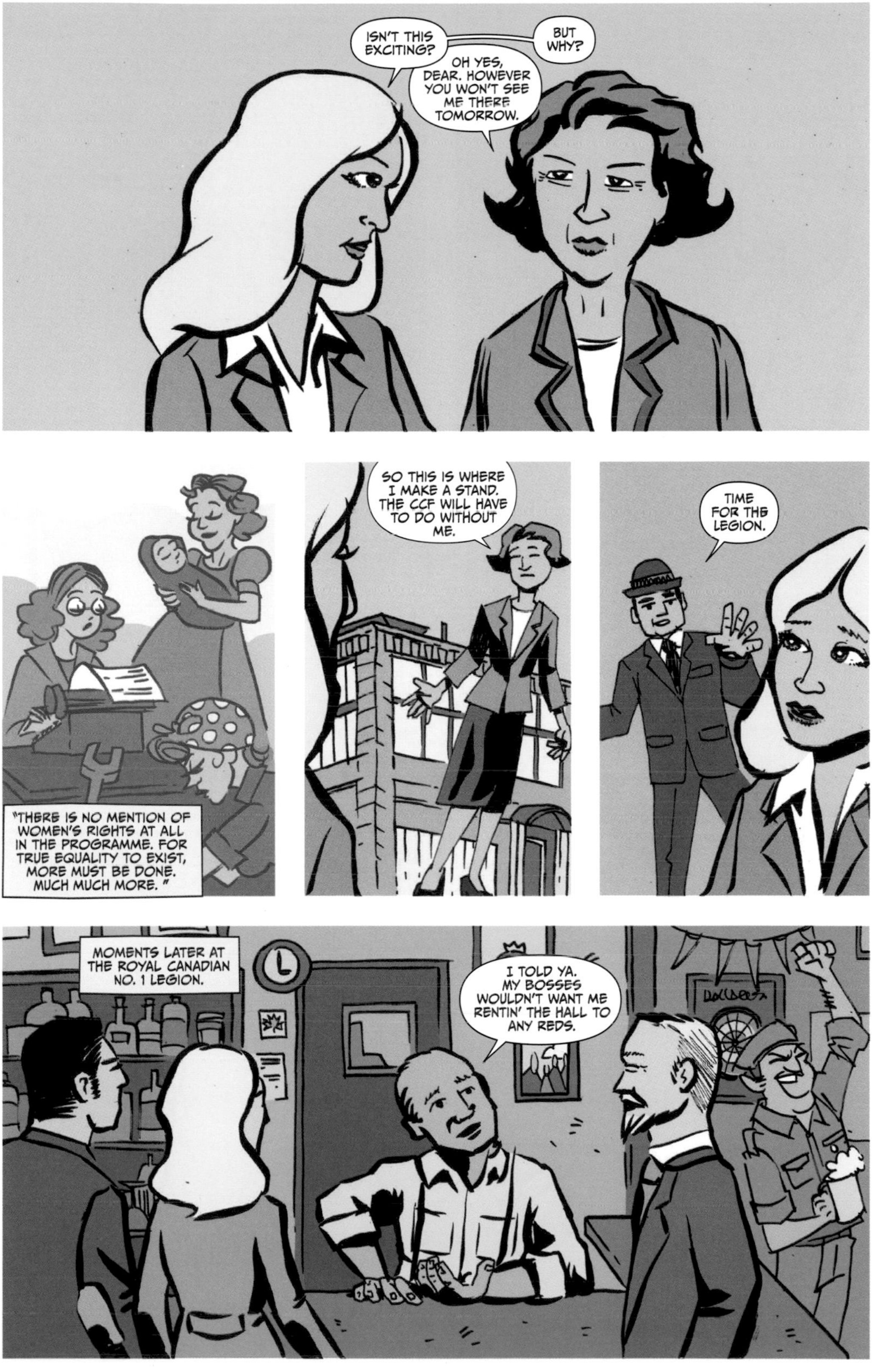
ISN'T THIS EXCITING?
OH YES, DEAR. HOWEVER YOU WON'T SEE ME THERE TOMORROW.
BUT WHY?
"THERE IS NO MENTION OF WOMEN'S RIGHTS AT ALL IN THE PROGRAMME. FOR TRUE EQUALITY TO EXIST, MORE MUST BE DONE. MUCH MUCH MORE."
SO THIS IS WHERE I MAKE A STAND. THE CCF WILL HAVE TO DO WITHOUT ME.
TIME FOR THE LEGION.
MOMENTS LATER AT THE ROYAL CANADIAN NO. 1 LEGION.
I TOLD YA. MY BOSSES WOULDN'T WANT ME RENTIN' THE HALL TO ANY REDS.

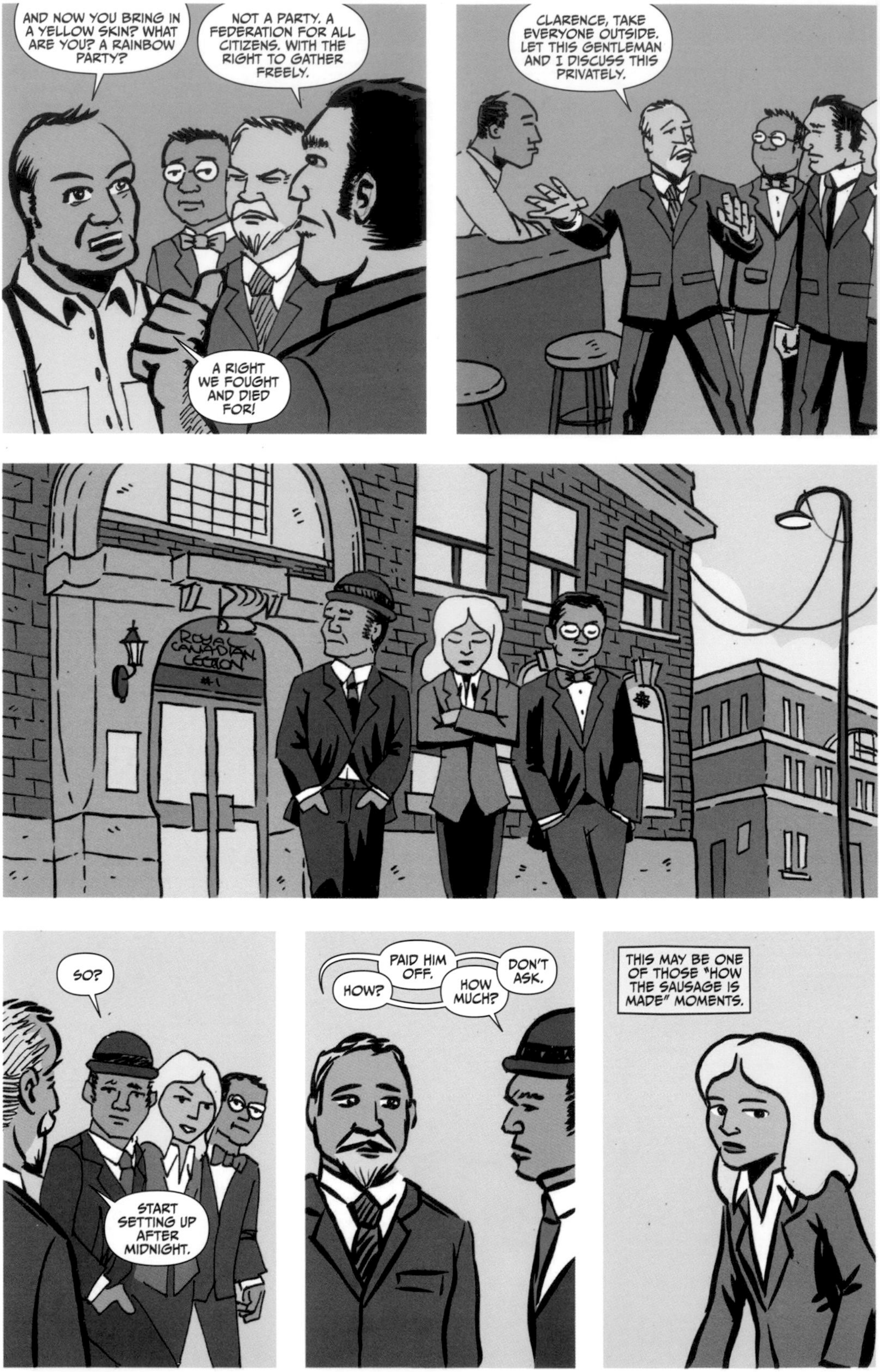
AND NOW YOU BRING IN A YELLOW SKIN? WHAT ARE YOU? A RAINBOW PARTY?
NOT A PARTY. A FEDERATION FOR ALL CITIZENS. WITH THE RIGHT TO GATHER FREELY.
A RIGHT WE FOUGHT AND DIED FOR!
CLARENCE, TAKE EVERYONE OUTSIDE. LET THIS GENTLEMAN AND I DISCUSS THIS PRIVATELY.
ROYAL CANADIAN LEGION
SO?
START SETTING UP AFTER MIDNIGHT.
HOW?
PAID HIM OFF.
HOW MUCH?
DON'T ASK.
THIS MAY BE ONE OF THOSE "HOW THE SAUSAGE IS MADE" MOMENTS.

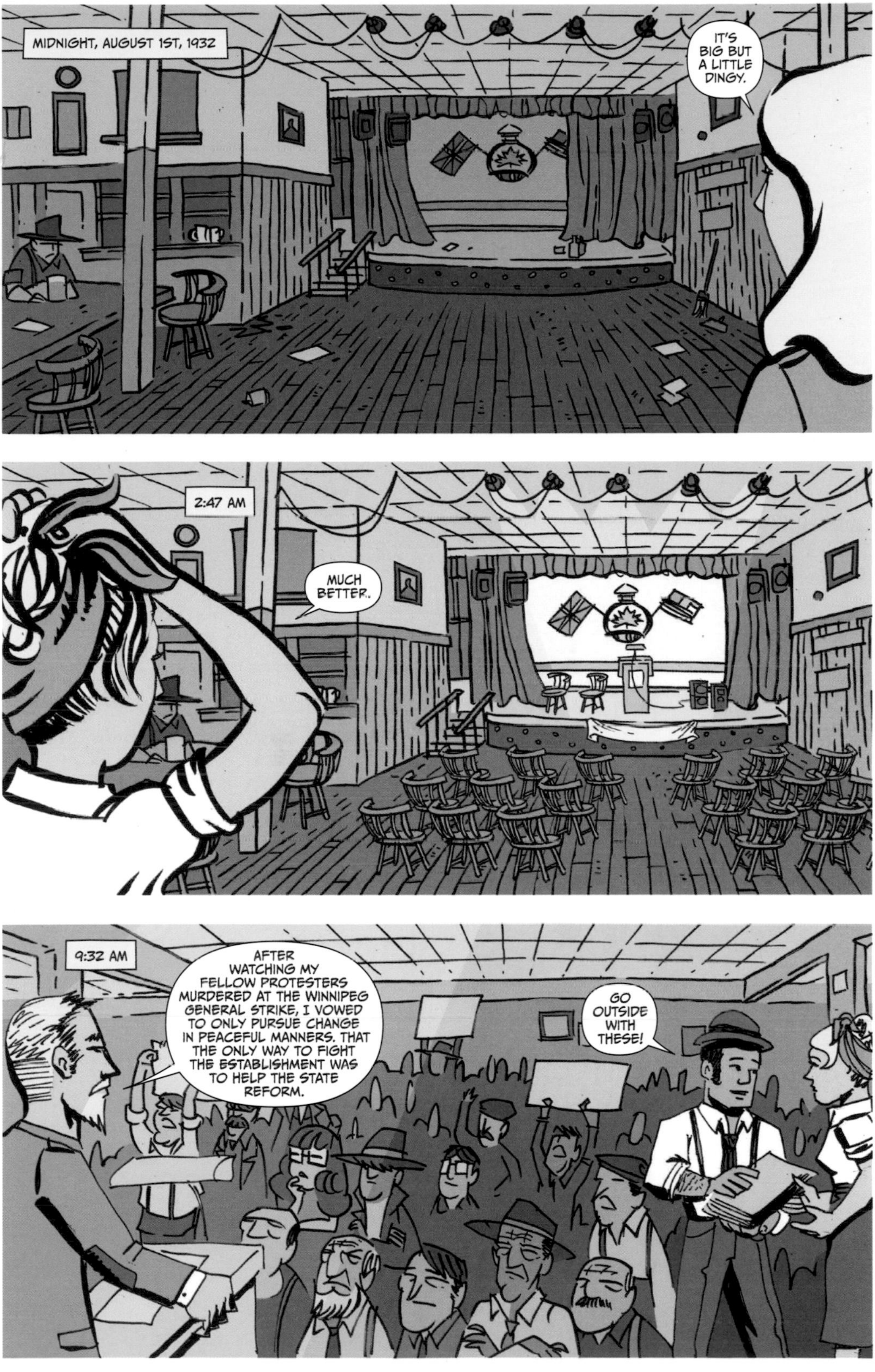
MIDNIGHT, AUGUST 1ST, 1932
IT'S BIG BUT A LITTLE DINGY.
2:47 AM
MUCH BETTER.
9:32 AM
AFTER WATCHING MY FELLOW PROTESTERS MURDERED AT THE WINNIPEG GENERAL STRIKE, I VOWED TO ONLY PURSUE CHANGE IN PEACEFUL MANNERS. THAT THE ONLY WAY TO FIGHT THE ESTABLISHMENT WAS TO HELP THE STATE REFORM.
GO OUTSIDE WITH THESE!

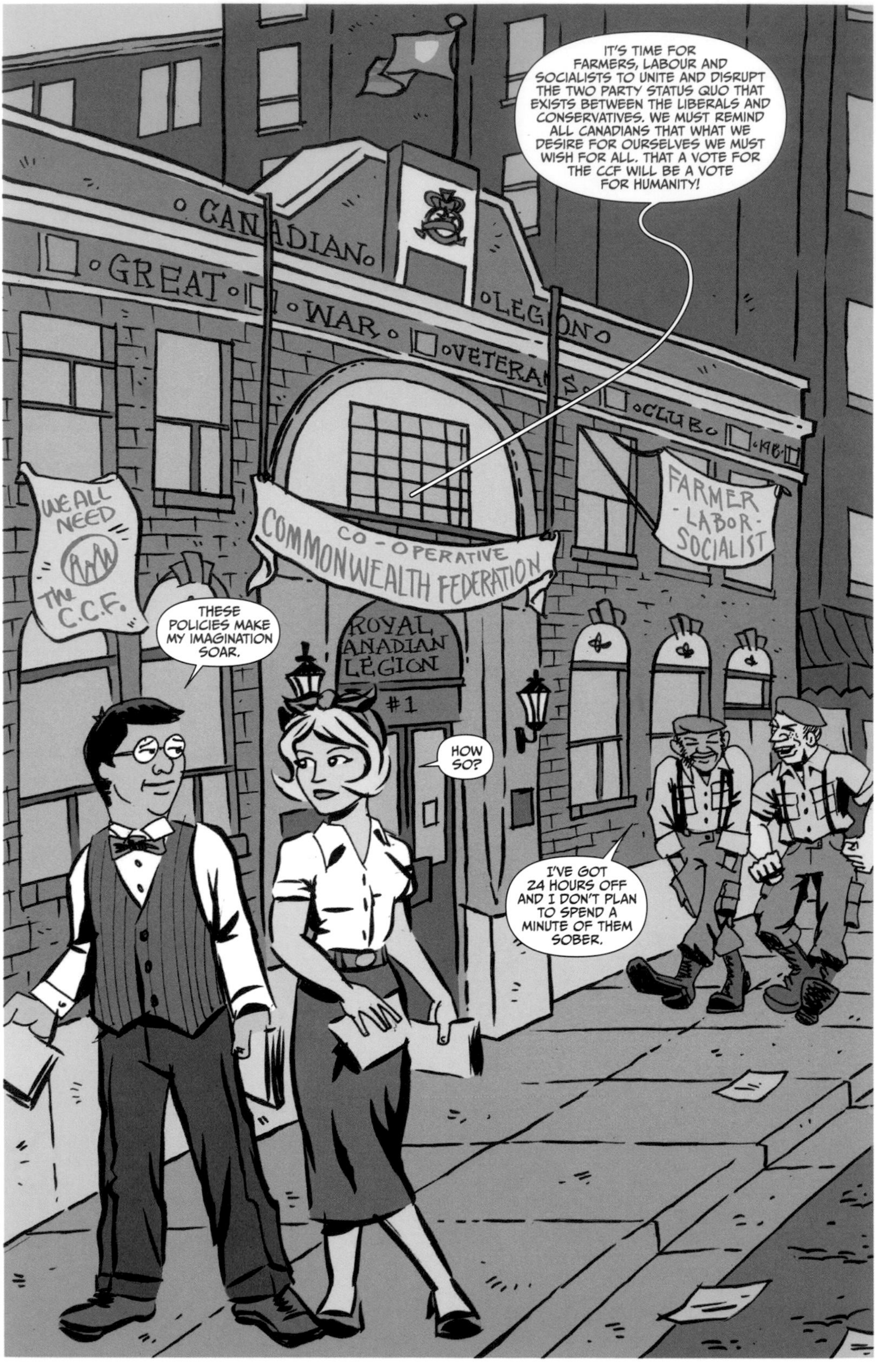
IT'S TIME FOR FARMERS, LABOUR AND SOCIALISTS TO UNITE AND DISRUPT THE TWO PARTY STATUS QUO THAT EXISTS BETWEEN THE LIBERALS AND CONSERVATIVES. WE MUST REMIND ALL CANADIANS THAT WHAT WE DESIRE FOR OURSELVES WE MUST WISH FOR ALL. THAT A VOTE FOR THE CCF WILL BE A VOTE FOR HUMANITY!
CANADIAN GREAT WAR VETERANS CLUB LEGION
WE ALL NEED THE C.C.F.
CO-OPERATIVE COMMONWEALTH FEDERATION
FARMER - LABOR - SOCIALIST
ROYAL CANADIAN LEGION #1
THESE POLICIES MAKE MY IMAGINATION SOAR.
HOW SO?
I'VE GOT 24 HOURS OFF AND I DON'T PLAN TO SPEND A MINUTE OF THEM SOBER.

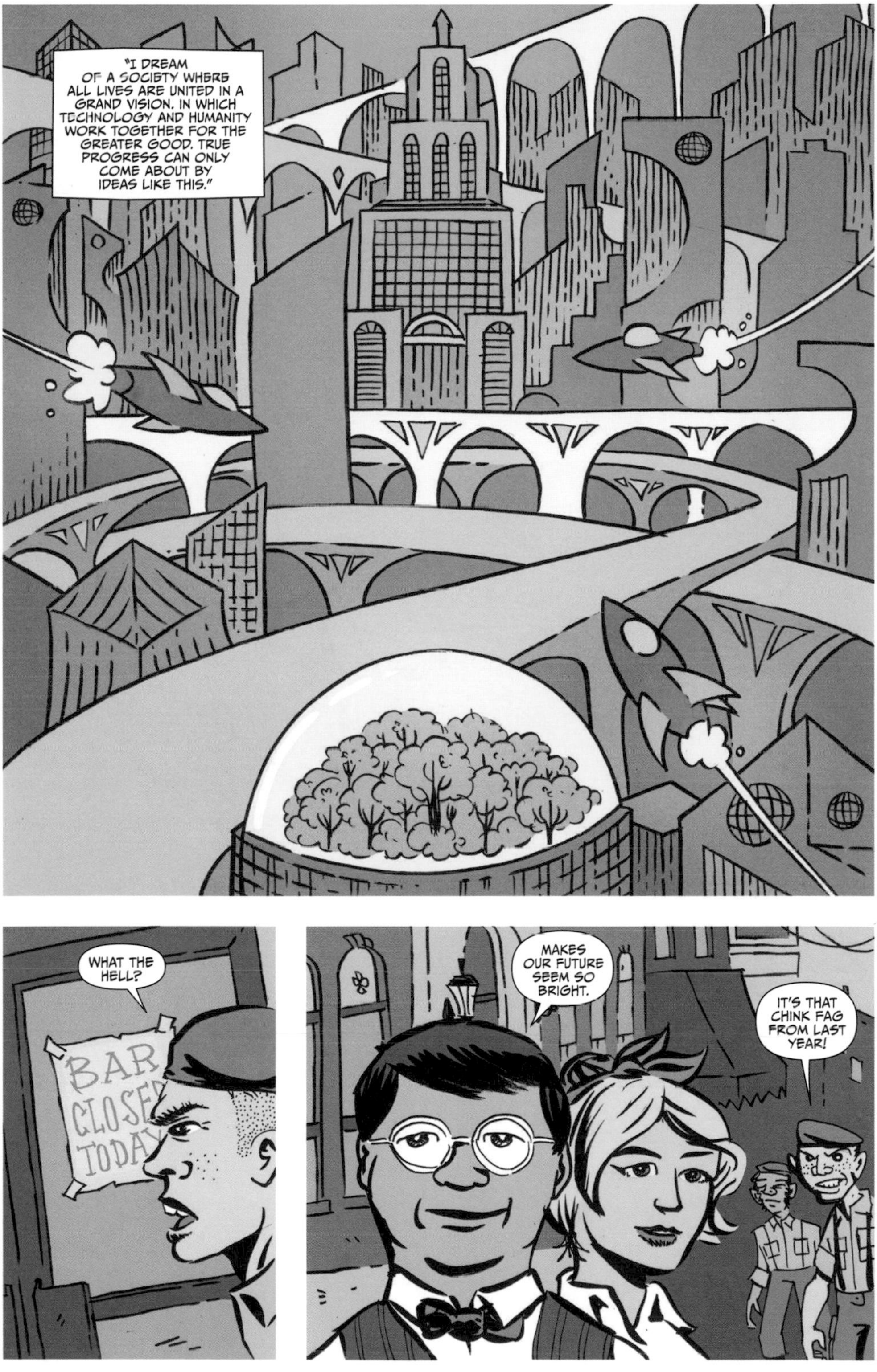
"I DREAM OF A SOCIETY WHERE ALL LIVES ARE UNITED IN A GRAND VISION. IN WHICH TECHNOLOGY AND HUMANITY WORK TOGETHER FOR THE GREATER GOOD. TRUE PROGRESS CAN ONLY COME ABOUT BY IDEAS LIKE THIS."
WHAT THE HELL?
BAR CLOSED TODAY
MAKES OUR FUTURE SEEM SO BRIGHT.
IT'S THAT CHINK FAG FROM LAST YEAR!

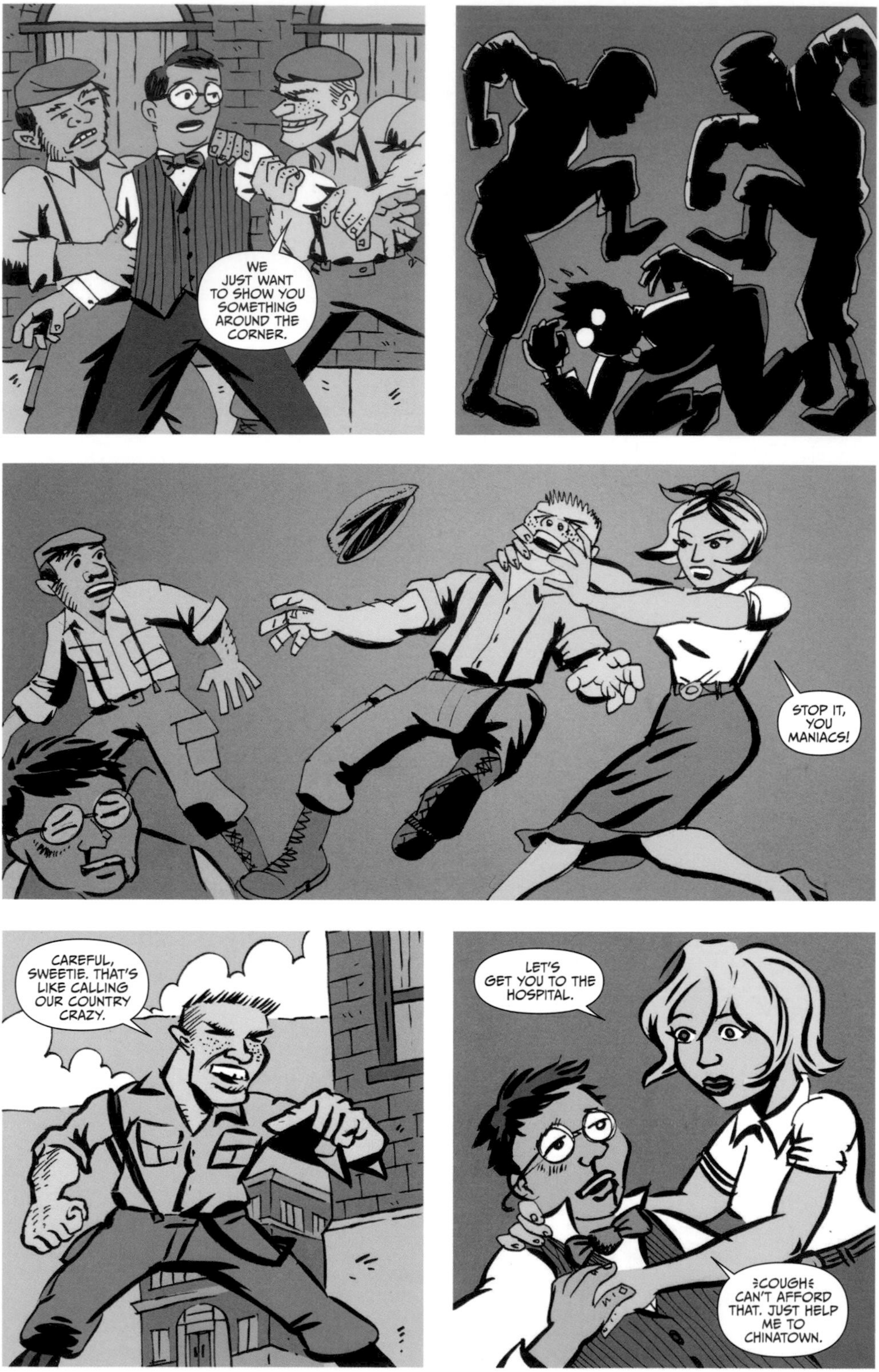
WE JUST WANT TO SHOW YOU SOMETHING AROUND THE CORNER.
STOP IT, YOU MANIACS!
CAREFUL, SWEETIE. THAT'S LIKE CALLING OUR COUNTRY CRAZY.
LET'S GET YOU TO THE HOSPITAL.
COUGH CAN'T AFFORD THAT. JUST HELP ME TO CHINATOWN.

PART III
GINSENG & SWEETGRASS

*"Fill your bowl to the brim
and it will spill.
Keep sharpening your knife
and it will blunt.
Chase after money and security
and your heart will never unclench.
Care about people's approval
and you will be their prisoner.
Do your work, then step back.
The only path to serenity."*

- Lao-Tzu

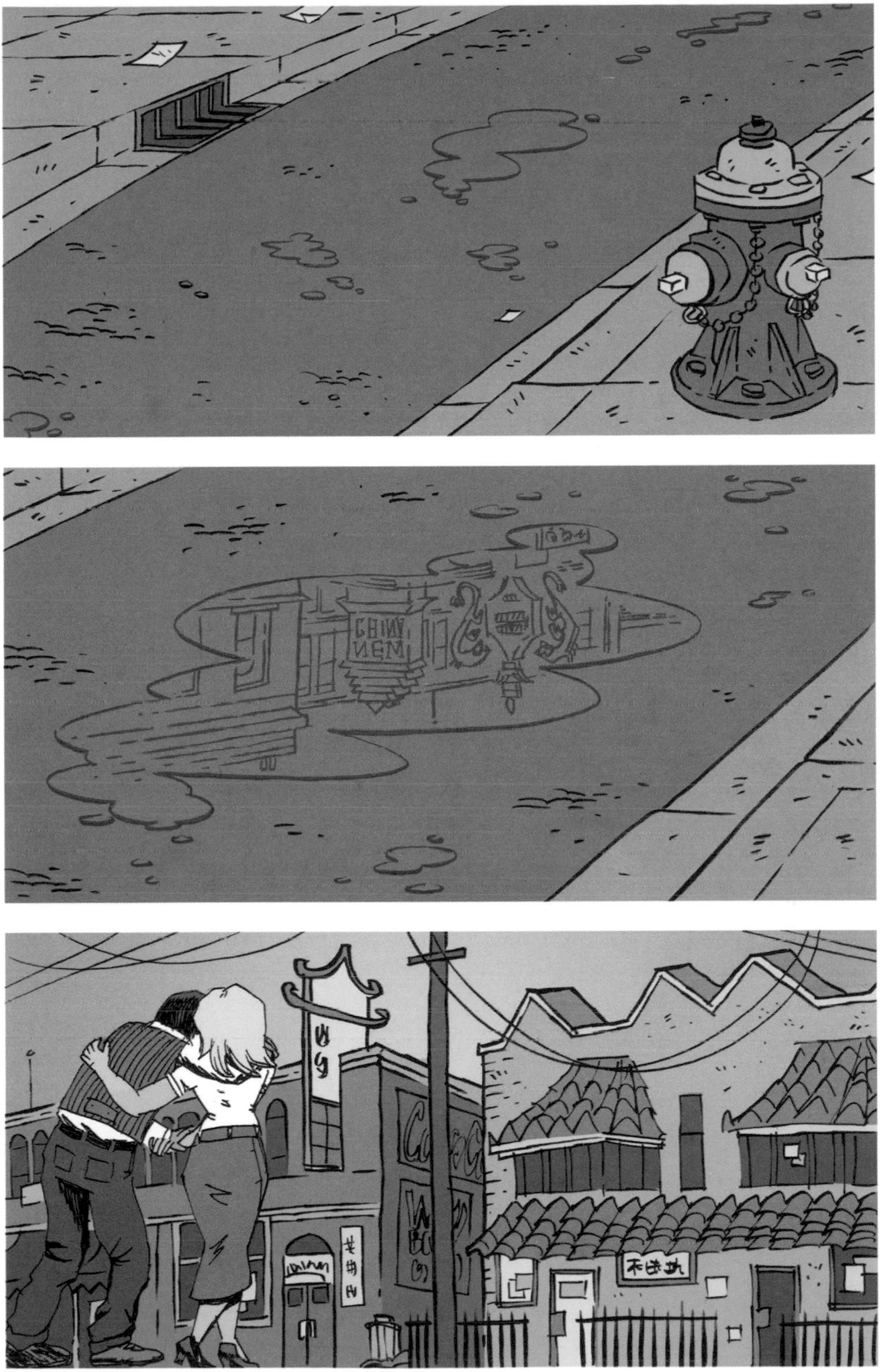

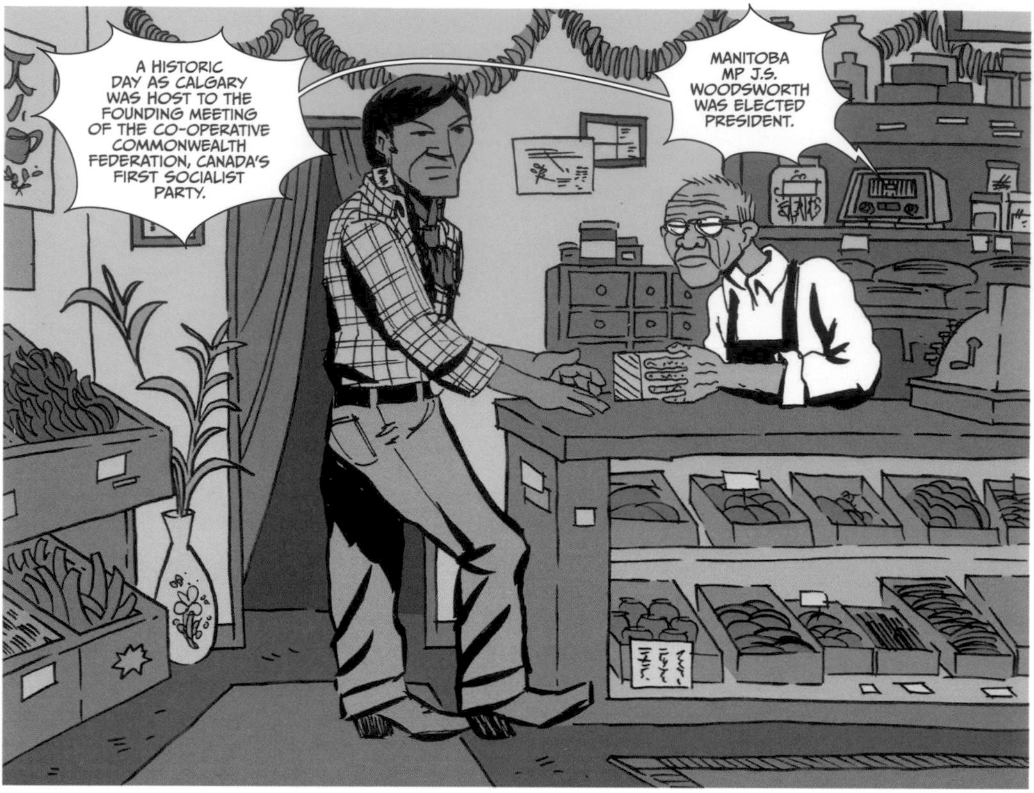
A HISTORIC DAY AS CALGARY WAS HOST TO THE FOUNDING MEETING OF THE CO-OPERATIVE COMMONWEALTH FEDERATION, CANADA'S FIRST SOCIALIST PARTY.
MANITOBA MP J.S. WOODSWORTH WAS ELECTED PRESIDENT.

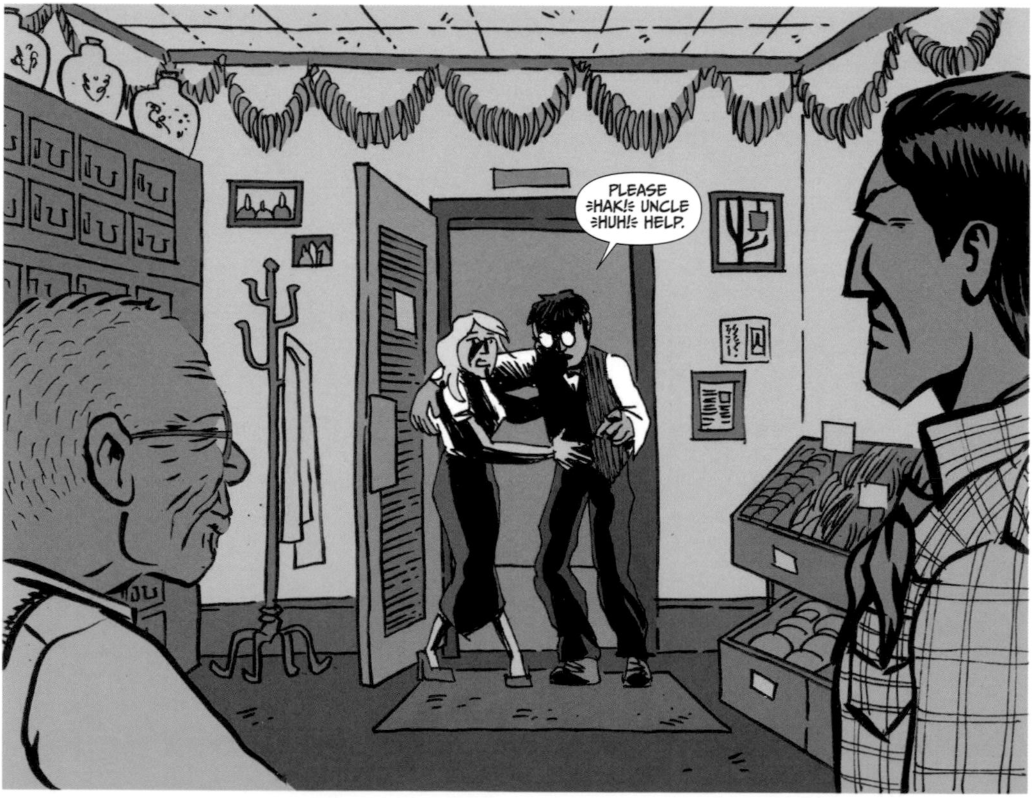
PLEASE =HAK!= UNCLE =HUH!= HELP.

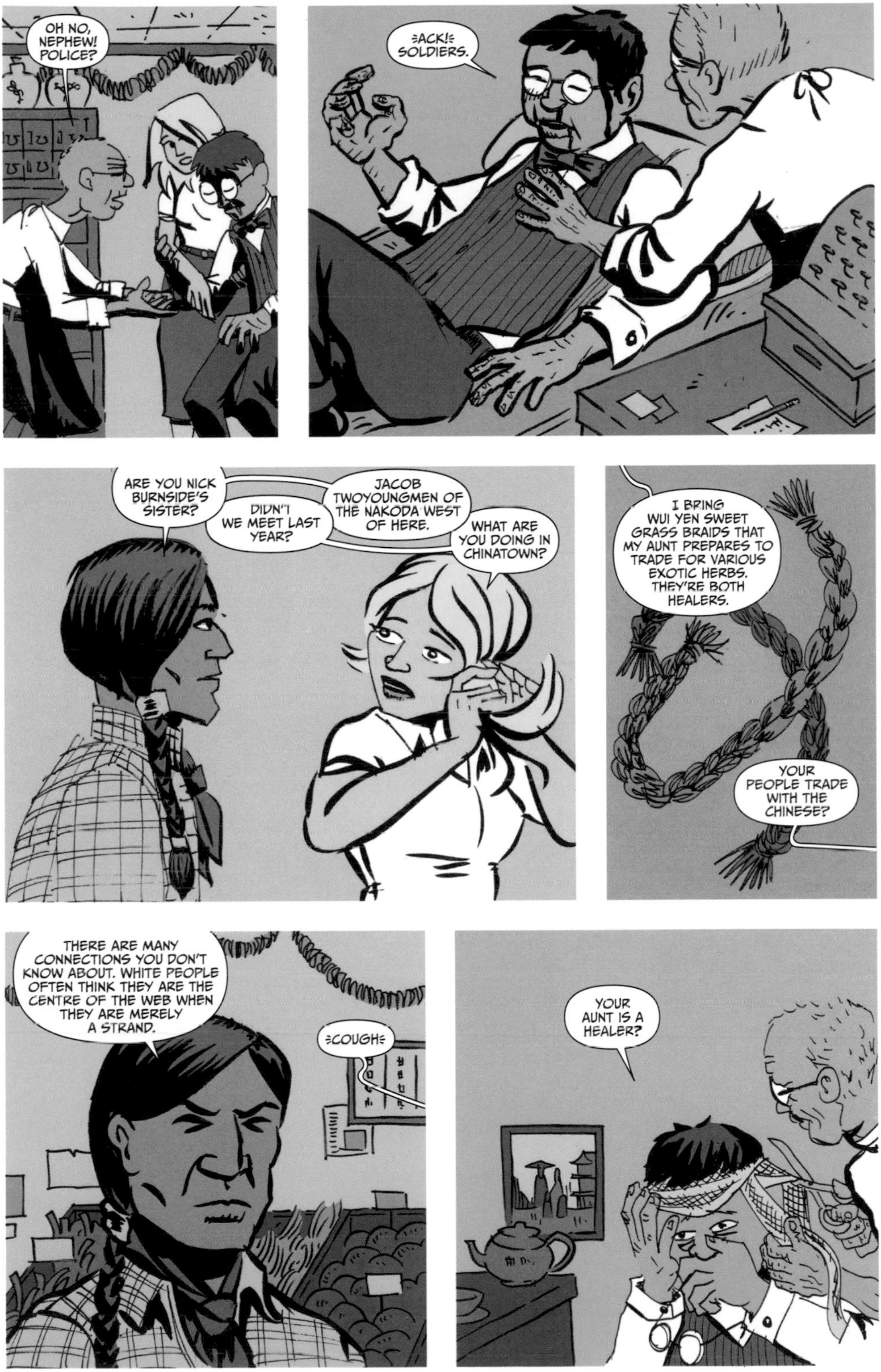
OH NO, NEPHEW! POLICE?
=ACK!= SOLDIERS.
ARE YOU NICK BURNSIDE'S SISTER?
DIDN'T WE MEET LAST YEAR?
JACOB TWOYOUNGMEN OF THE NAKODA WEST OF HERE.
WHAT ARE YOU DOING IN CHINATOWN?
I BRING WUI YEN SWEET GRASS BRAIDS THAT MY AUNT PREPARES TO TRADE FOR VARIOUS EXOTIC HERBS. THEY'RE BOTH HEALERS.
YOUR PEOPLE TRADE WITH THE CHINESE?
THERE ARE MANY CONNECTIONS YOU DON'T KNOW ABOUT. WHITE PEOPLE OFTEN THINK THEY ARE THE CENTRE OF THE WEB WHEN THEY ARE MERELY A STRAND.
=COUGH=
YOUR AUNT IS A HEALER?

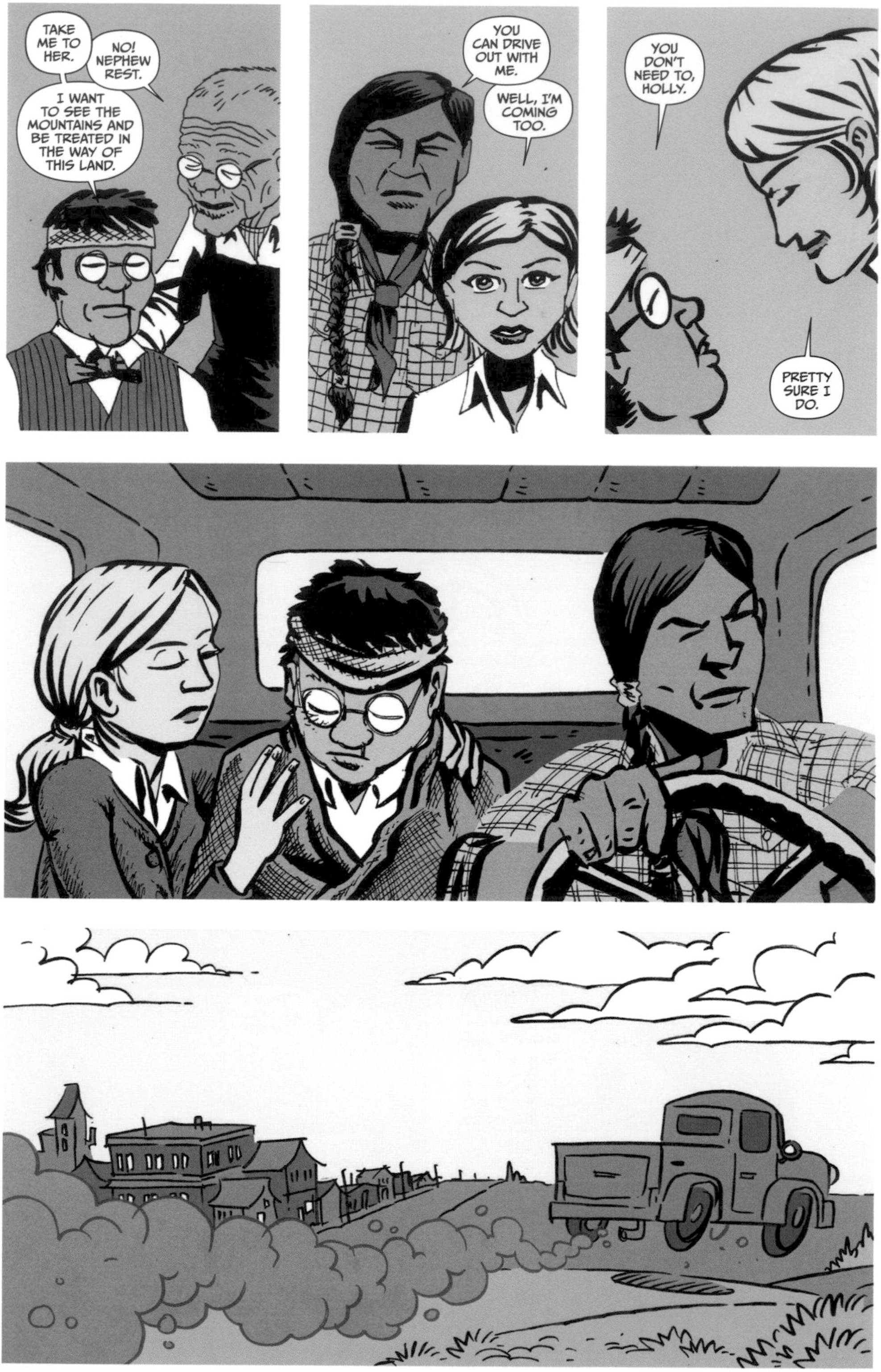
TAKE ME TO HER.
NO! NEPHEW REST.
I WANT TO SEE THE MOUNTAINS AND BE TREATED IN THE WAY OF THIS LAND.
YOU CAN DRIVE OUT WITH ME.
WELL, I'M COMING TOO.
YOU DON'T NEED TO, HOLLY.
PRETTY SURE I DO.

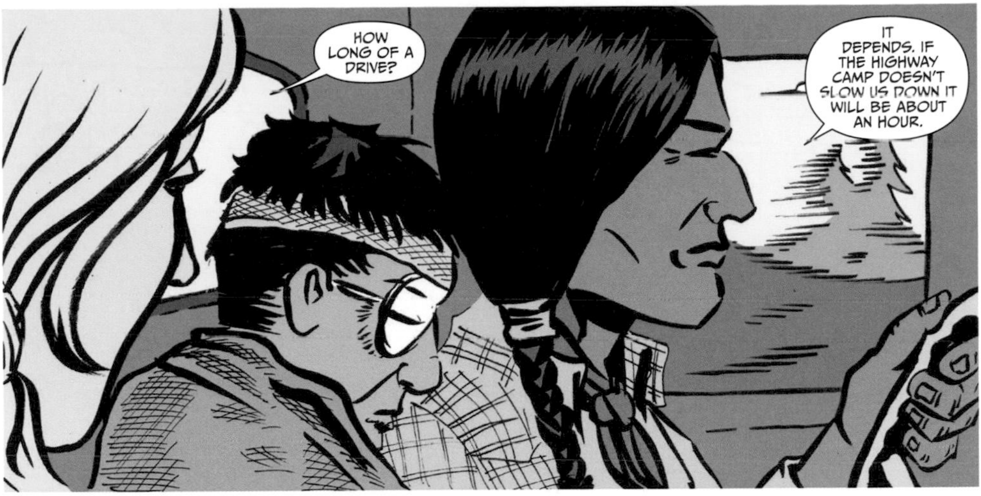
HOW LONG OF A DRIVE?
IT DEPENDS. IF THE HIGHWAY CAMP DOESN'T SLOW US DOWN IT WILL BE ABOUT AN HOUR.

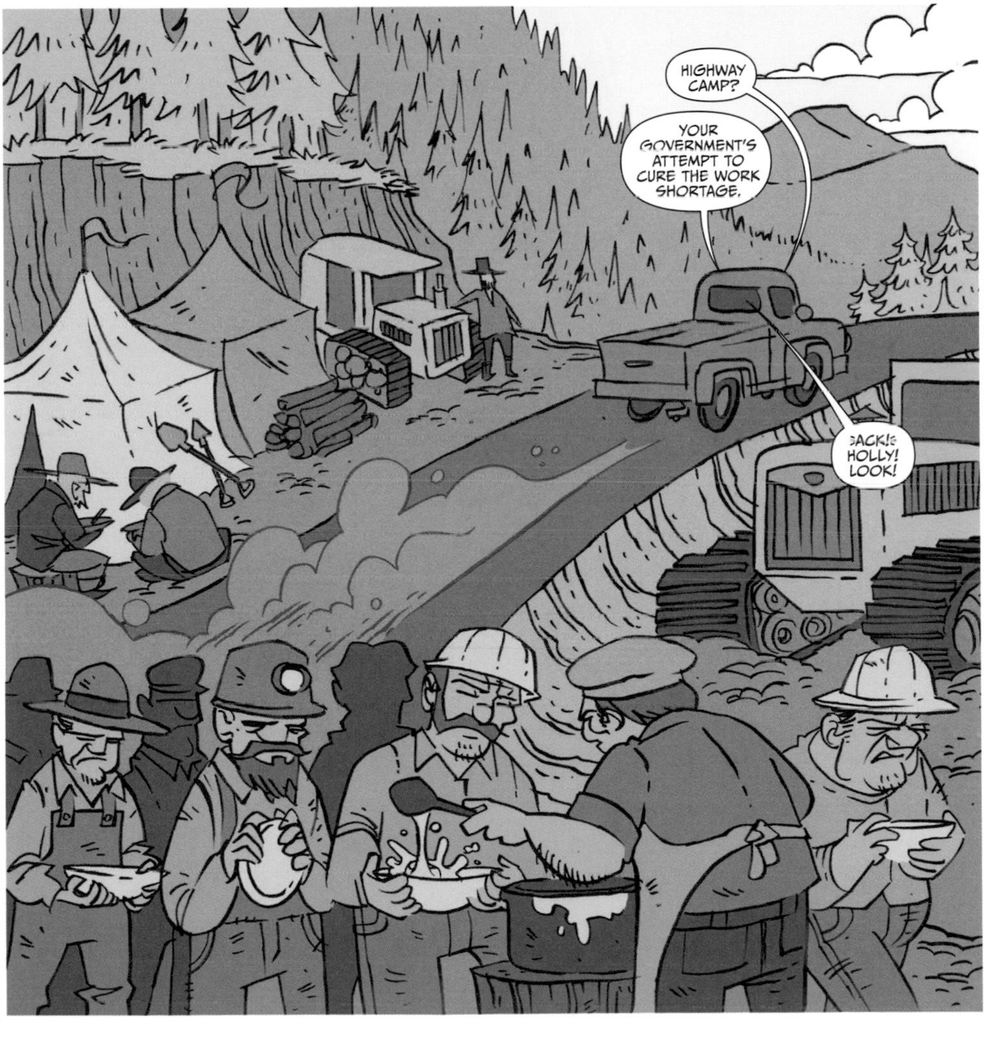
HIGHWAY CAMP?
YOUR GOVERNMENT'S ATTEMPT TO CURE THE WORK SHORTAGE.
JACKIE! HOLLY! LOOK!

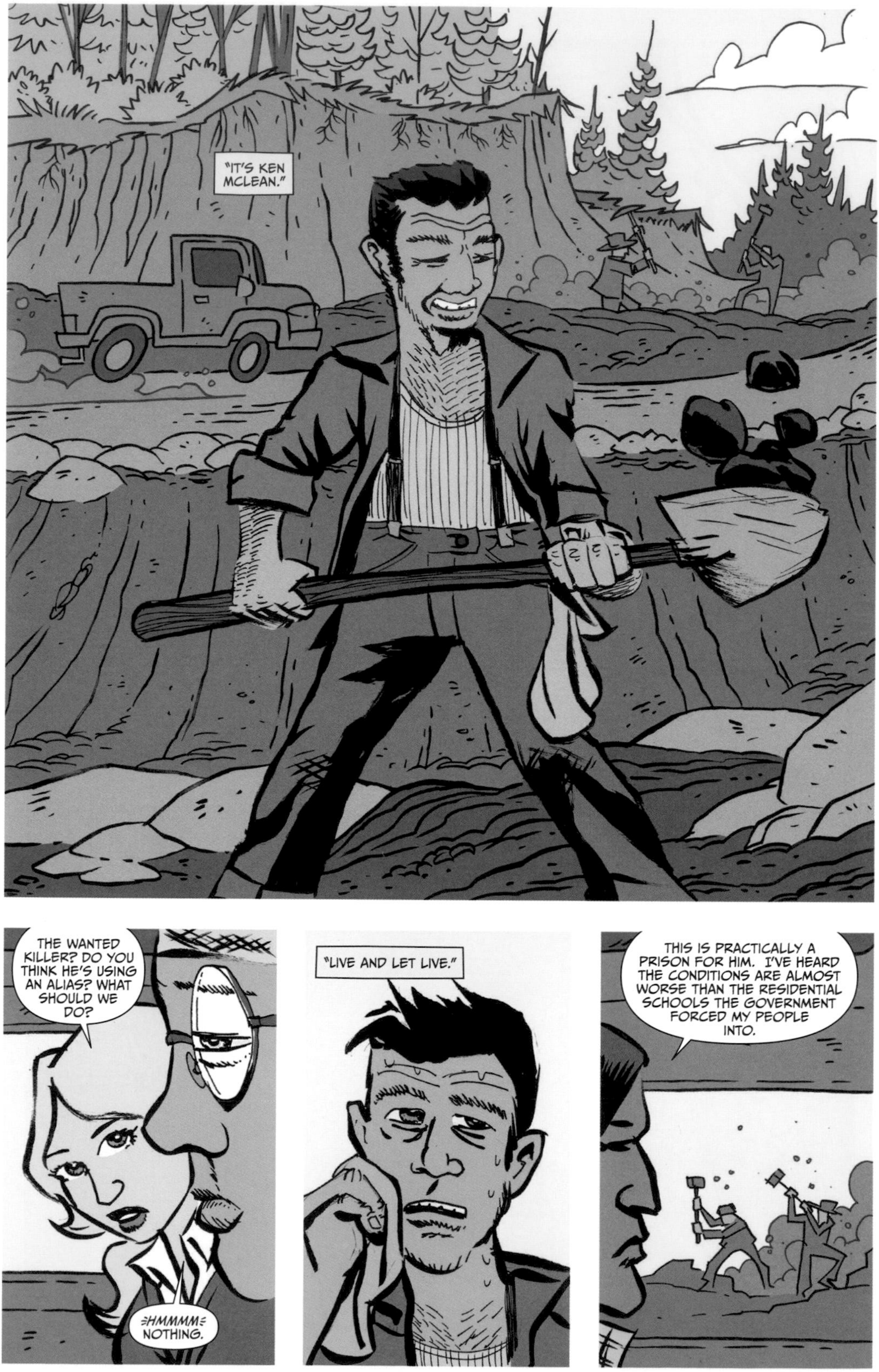
"IT'S KEN MCLEAN."
THE WANTED KILLER? DO YOU THINK HE'S USING AN ALIAS? WHAT SHOULD WE DO?
HMMMM NOTHING.
"LIVE AND LET LIVE."
THIS IS PRACTICALLY A PRISON FOR HIM. I'VE HEARD THE CONDITIONS ARE ALMOST WORSE THAN THE RESIDENTIAL SCHOOLS THE GOVERNMENT FORCED MY PEOPLE INTO.

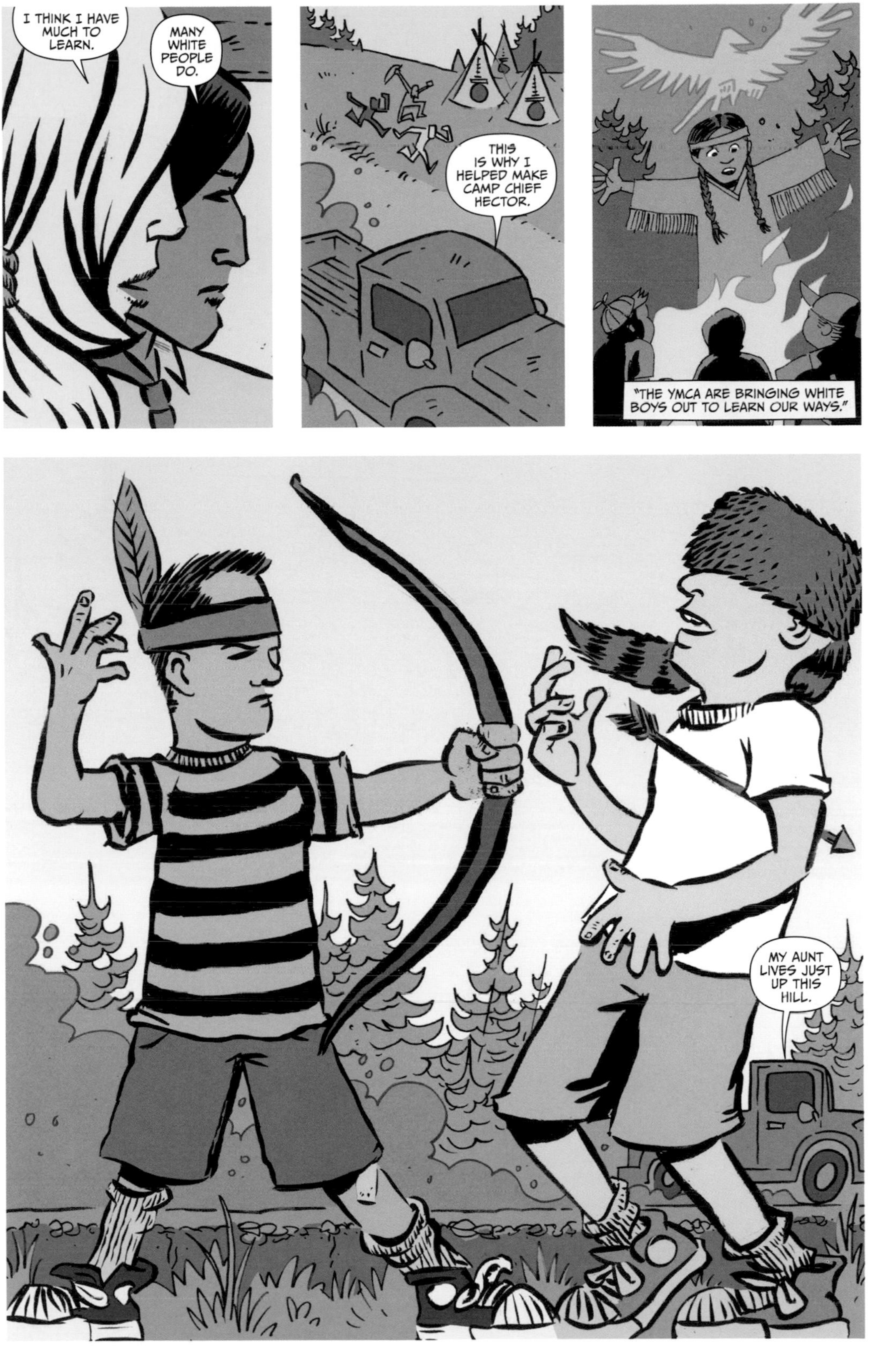
I THINK I HAVE MUCH TO LEARN.
MANY WHITE PEOPLE DO.
THIS IS WHY I HELPED MAKE CAMP CHIEF HECTOR.
"THE YMCA ARE BRINGING WHITE BOYS OUT TO LEARN OUR WAYS."
MY AUNT LIVES JUST UP THIS HILL.

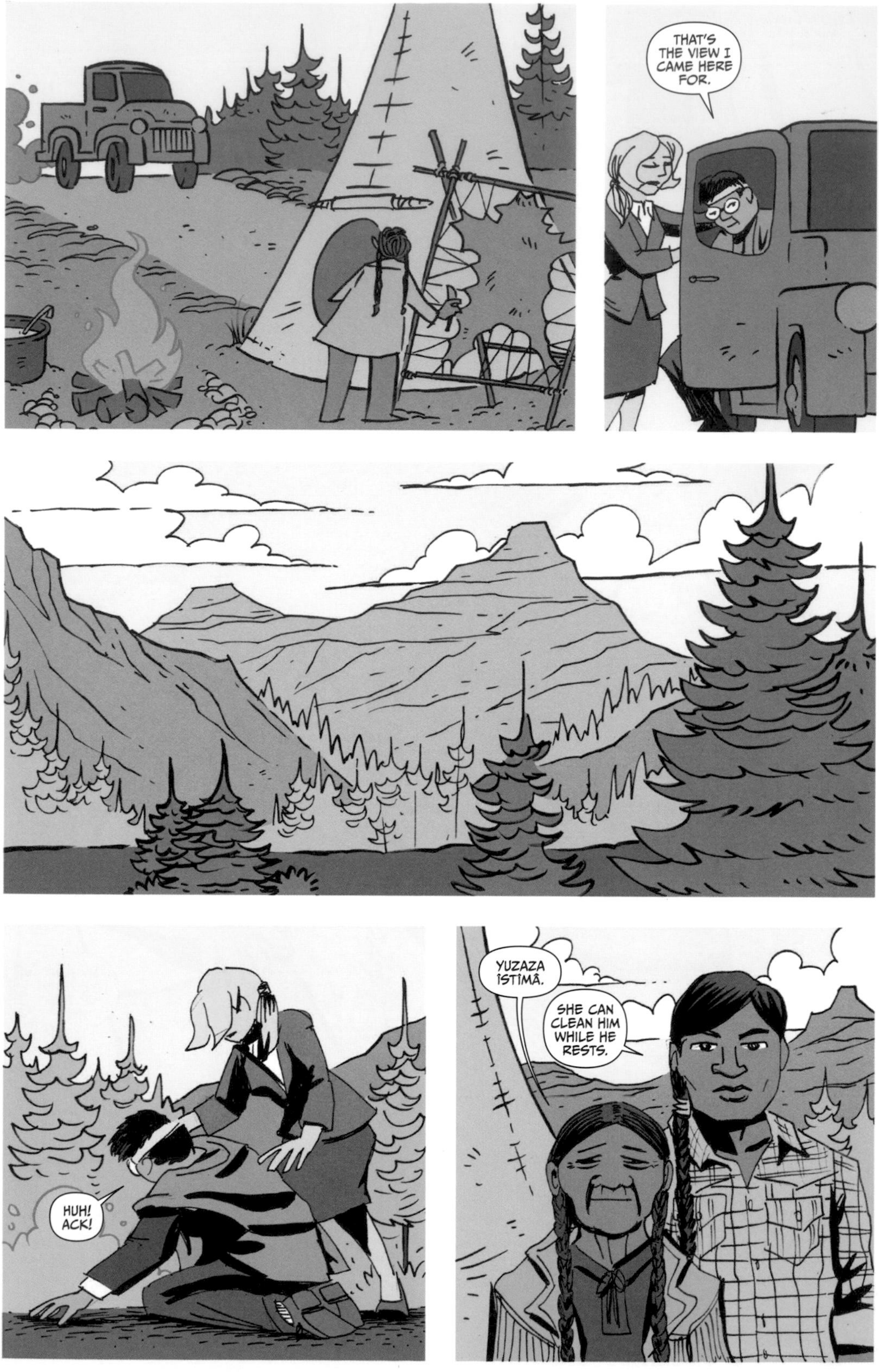
THAT'S THE VIEW I CAME HERE FOR.
HUH! ACK!
YUZAZA ÎSTIMÂ.
SHE CAN CLEAN HIM WHILE HE RESTS.

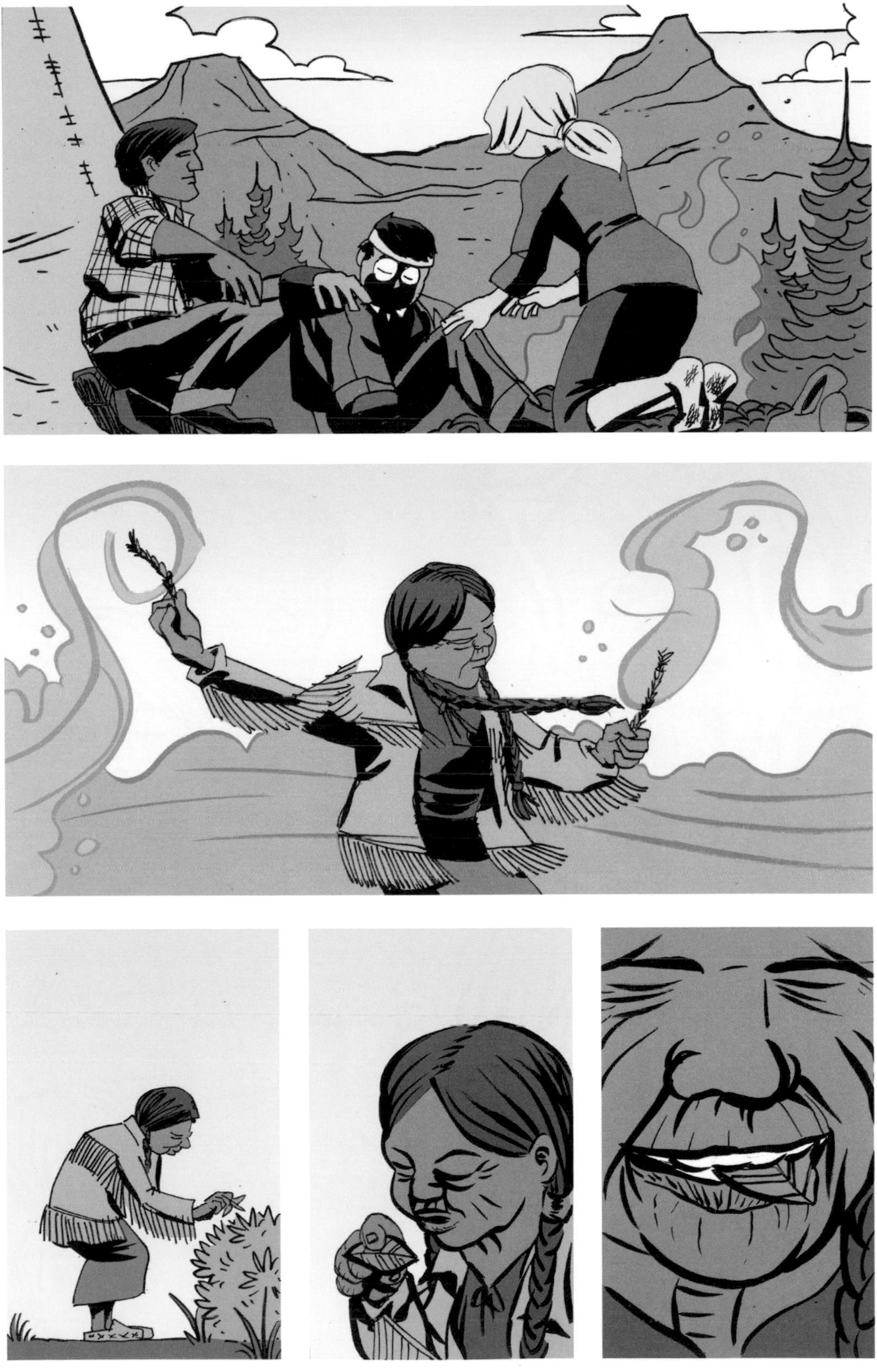

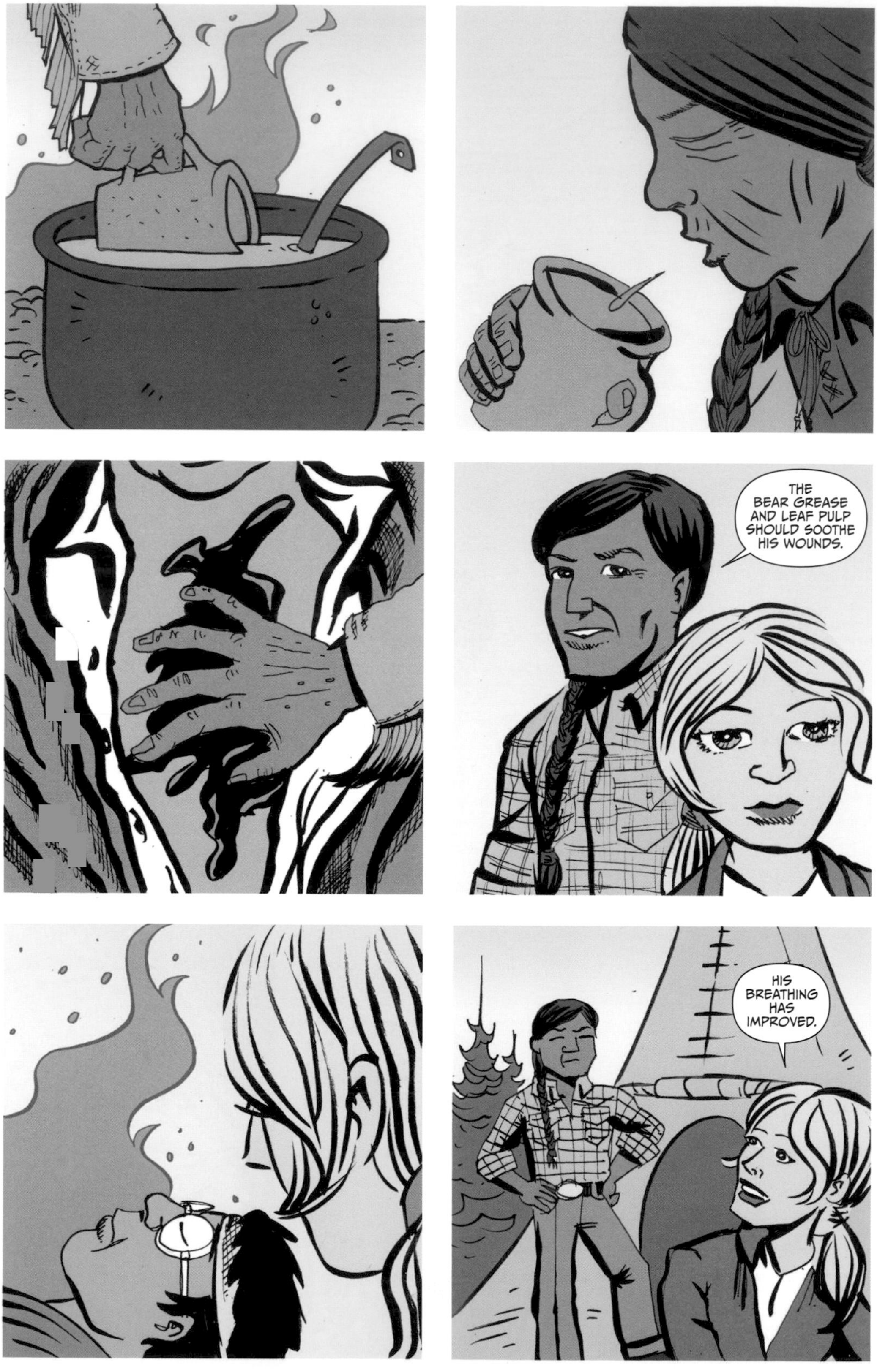
THE BEAR GREASE AND LEAF PULP SHOULD SOOTHE HIS WOUNDS.
HIS BREATHING HAS IMPROVED.

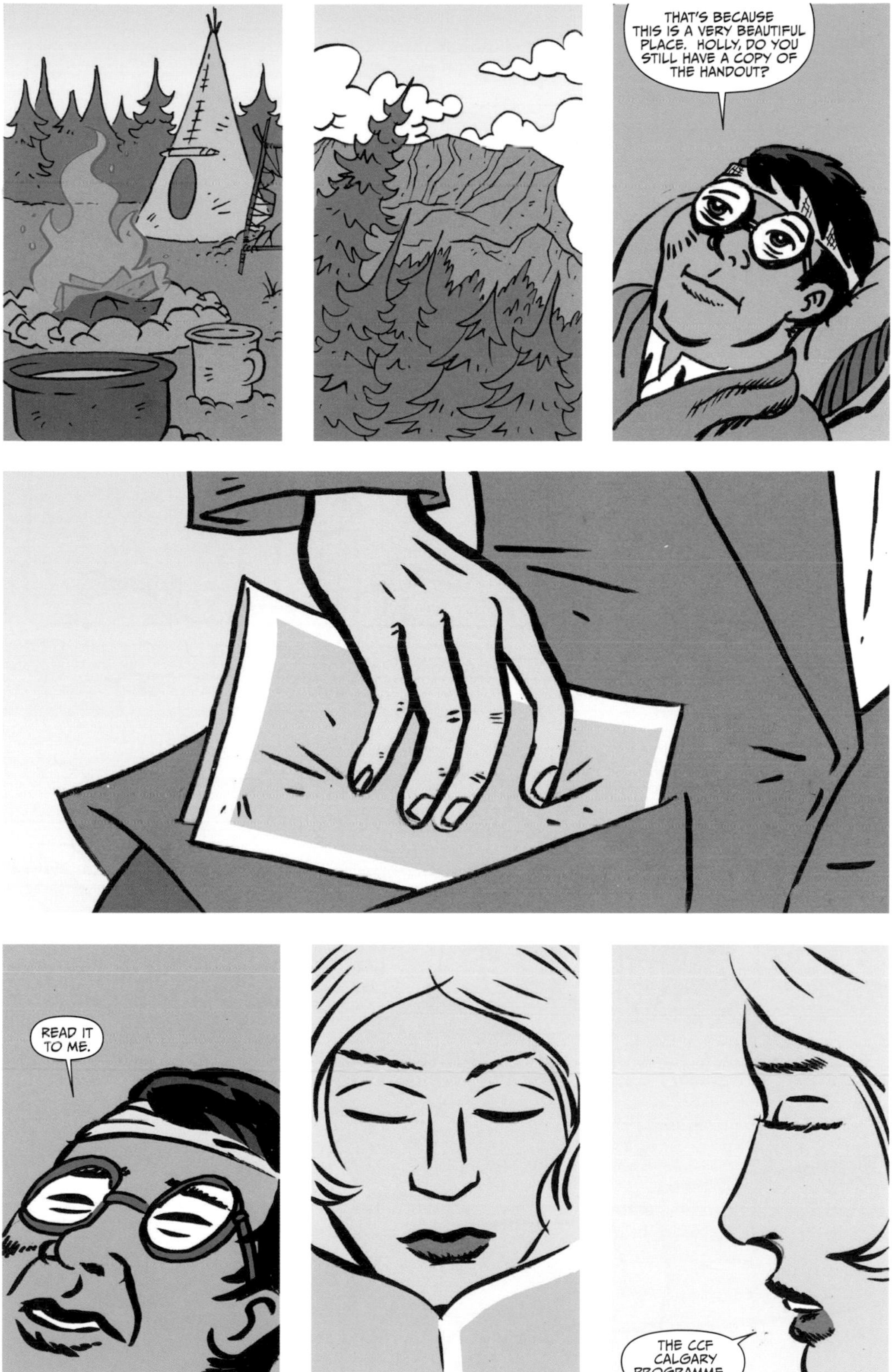
THAT'S BECAUSE THIS IS A VERY BEAUTIFUL PLACE. HOLLY, DO YOU STILL HAVE A COPY OF THE HANDOUT?
READ IT TO ME.
THE CCF CALGARY PROGRAMME...

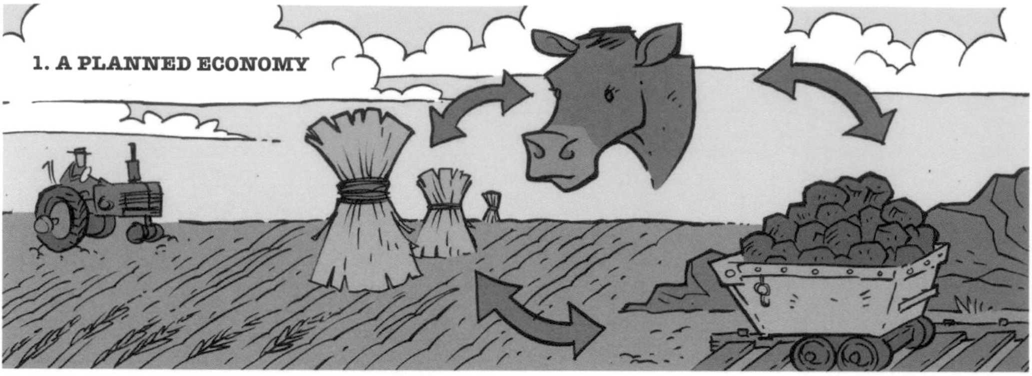
1. A PLANNED ECONOMY

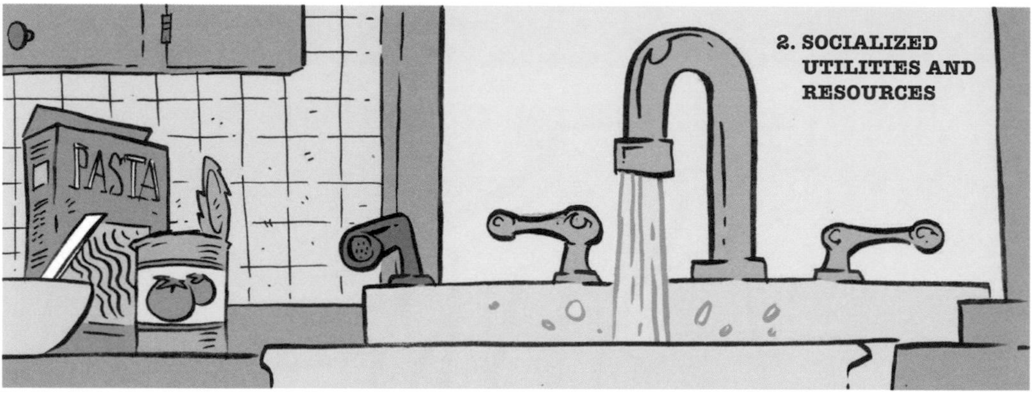
2. SOCIALIZED UTILITIES AND RESOURCES
PASTA

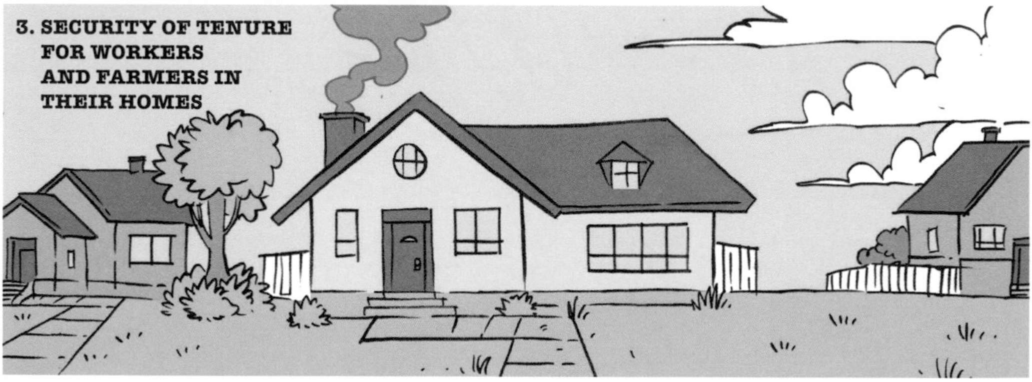
3. SECURITY OF TENURE FOR WORKERS AND FARMERS IN THEIR HOMES

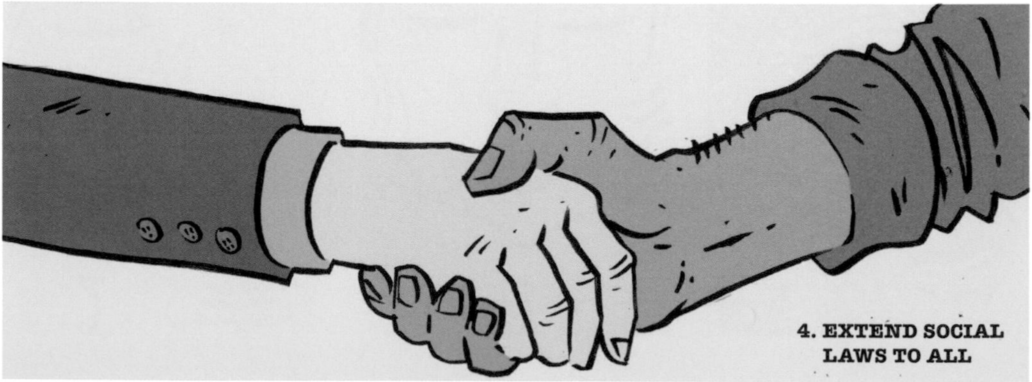
4. EXTEND SOCIAL LAWS TO ALL

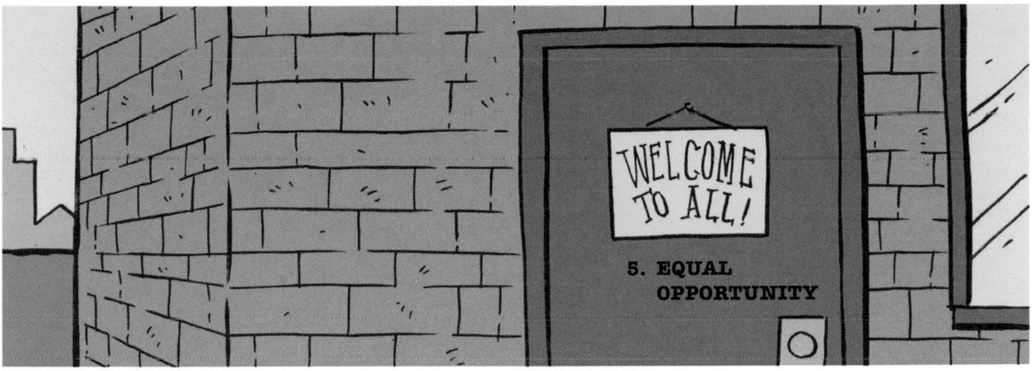
WELCOME TO ALL!
5. EQUAL OPPORTUNITY

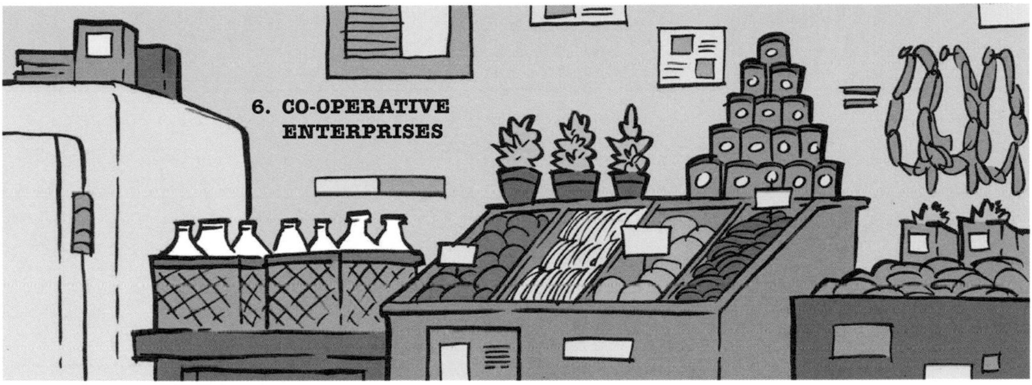
6. CO-OPERATIVE ENTERPRISES

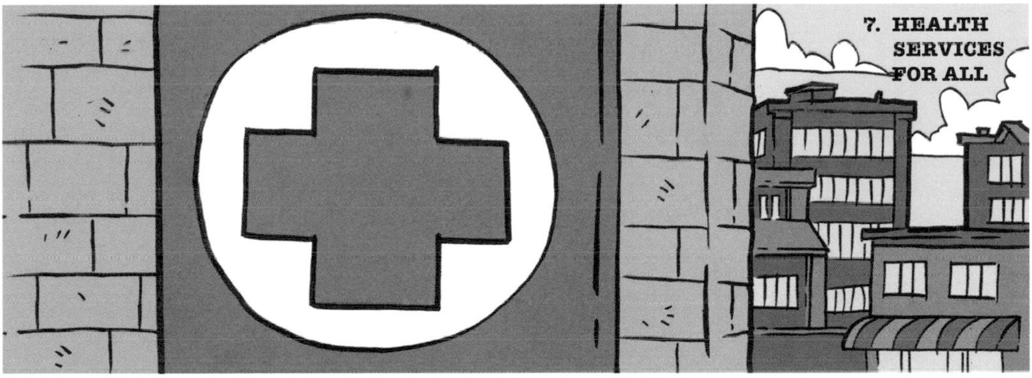
7. HEALTH SERVICES FOR ALL

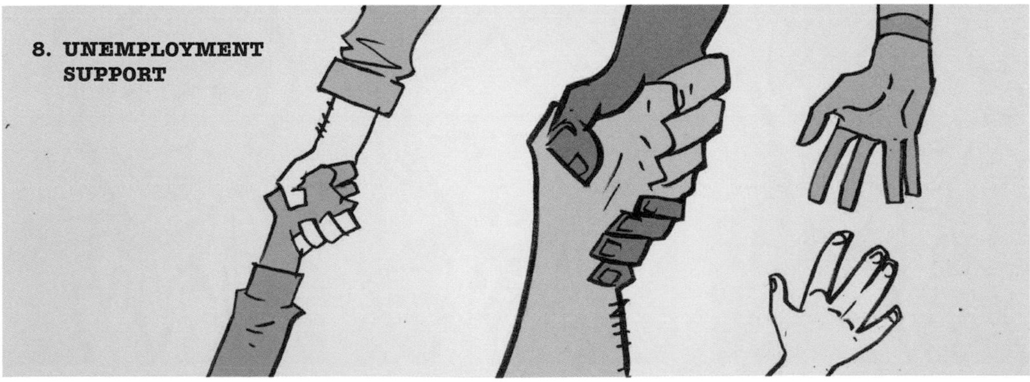
8. UNEMPLOYMENT SUPPORT

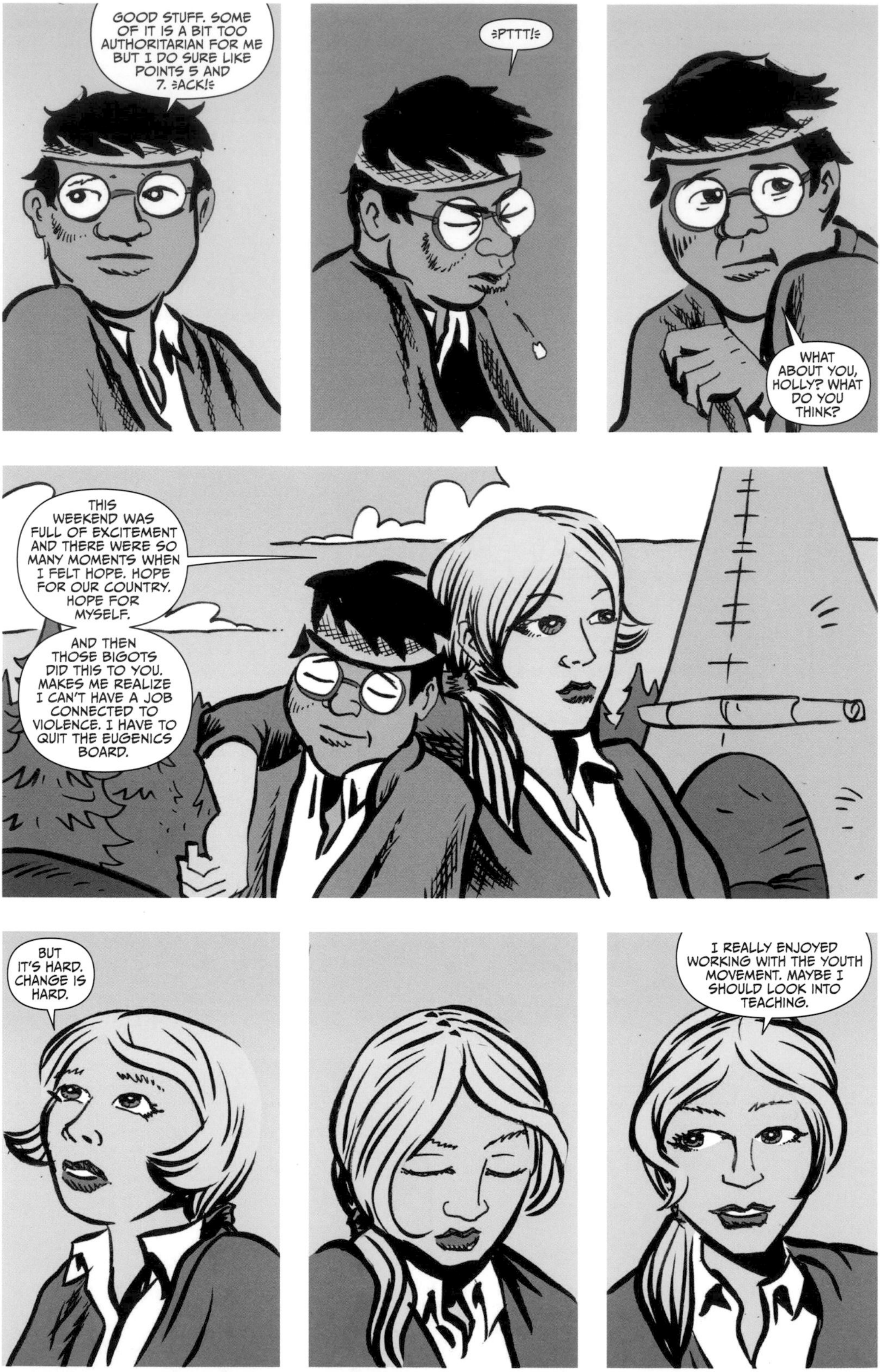
GOOD STUFF. SOME OF IT IS A BIT TOO AUTHORITARIAN FOR ME BUT I DO SURE LIKE POINTS 5 AND 7. ≡ACK!≡
≡PTTT!≡
WHAT ABOUT YOU, HOLLY? WHAT DO YOU THINK?
THIS WEEKEND WAS FULL OF EXCITEMENT AND THERE WERE SO MANY MOMENTS WHEN I FELT HOPE. HOPE FOR OUR COUNTRY. HOPE FOR MYSELF.
AND THEN THOSE BIGOTS DID THIS TO YOU. MAKES ME REALIZE I CAN'T HAVE A JOB CONNECTED TO VIOLENCE. I HAVE TO QUIT THE EUGENICS BOARD.
BUT IT'S HARD. CHANGE IS HARD.
I REALLY ENJOYED WORKING WITH THE YOUTH MOVEMENT. MAYBE I SHOULD LOOK INTO TEACHING.

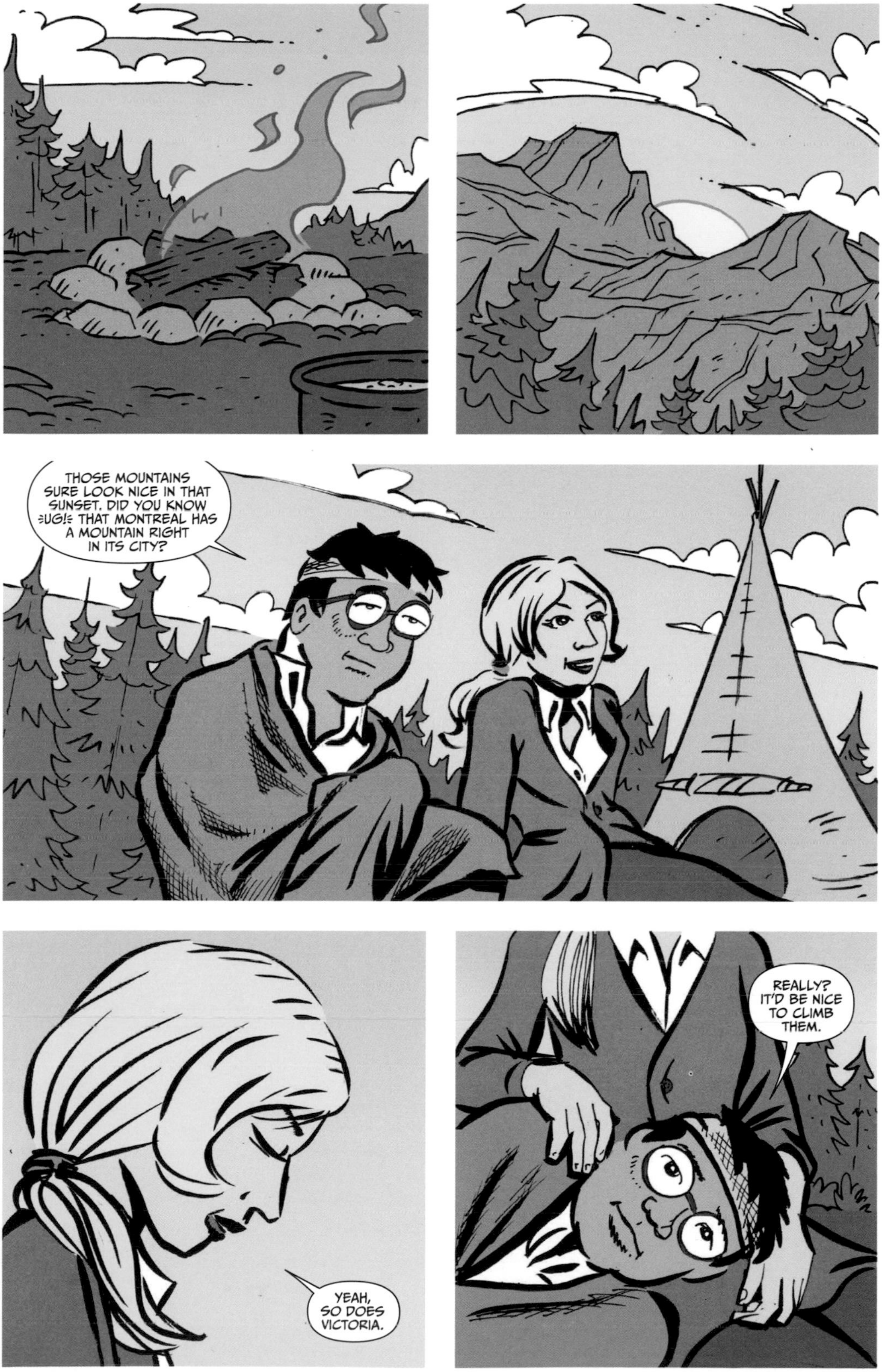
THOSE MOUNTAINS SURE LOOK NICE IN THAT SUNSET. DID YOU KNOW *UG!* THAT MONTREAL HAS A MOUNTAIN RIGHT IN ITS CITY?
YEAH, SO DOES VICTORIA.
REALLY? IT'D BE NICE TO CLIMB THEM.

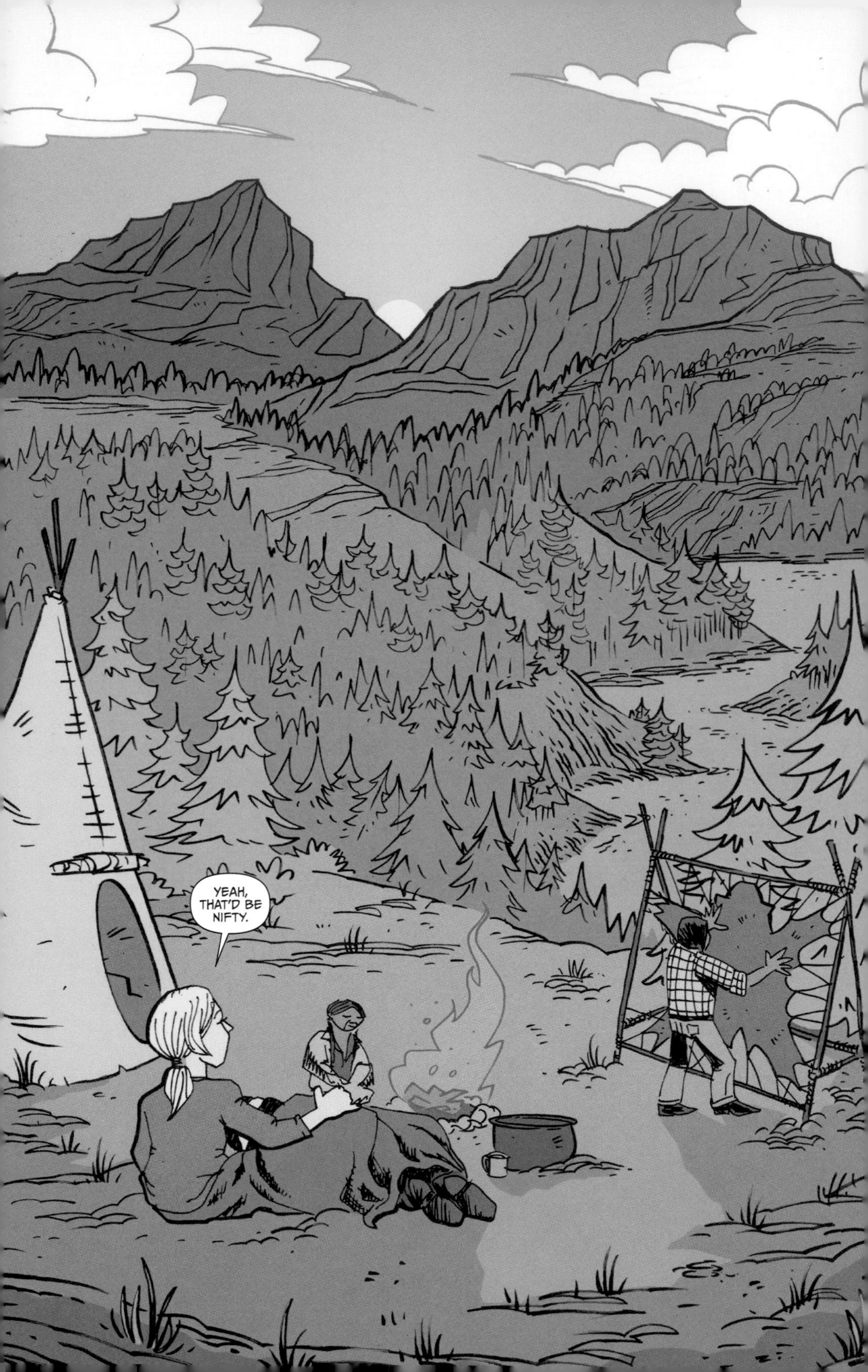
YEAH, THAT'D BE NIFTY.